DATE DUE

DEMCO 138298

SEABORN

TO MARY ROSE AND MATTHEW

Text copyright © 2008 by Craig Moodie

Published by Roaring Brook Press
Roaring Brook Press is a division of Holtzbrinck
Publishing Holdings Limited Partnership
175 Fifth Avenue, New York, NY 10010

www.roaringbrookpress.com

Distributed in Canada by H. B. Fenn and Company, Ltd.

Library of Congress Cataloging-in-Publication Data

Moodie, Craig.
Seaborn / Craig Moodie. — 1st ed.
p.   cm.
Summary: Craving "the Big Freedom," sixteen-year-old Luke resents
being cooped up with his father on a small sailboat just after his
mother walked out on them, but a sudden storm sweeps his father
overboard, leaving Luke to figure out how to survive on a damaged
boat in the Gulf Stream while dealing with his feelings of guilt.
ISBN-13: 978-1-59643-390-8
ISBN-10: 1-59643-390-6
[1. Fathers and sons—Fiction. 2. Shipwrecks—Fiction. 3. Survival—Fiction.
4. Sailing—Fiction. 5. Boats and boating—Fiction. 6. Artists—Fiction.
7. Family problems—Ficiton. 8. Gulf Stream—Fiction.] I. Title.
PZ7.M7723Sed 2008
[Fic]—dc22   2008011136

2 4 6 8 10 9 7 5 3 1

Roaring Brook Press books are available for special promotions and premiums.
For details, contact: Director of Special Markets, Holtzbrinck Publishers.

Book design by Mîkael Vilhjálmsson
Printed in the United States of America
First edition August 2008

SEA-BORN

A NOVEL BY
CRAIG MOODIE

ROARING BROOK PRESS
NEW YORK

The North Atlantic Ocean

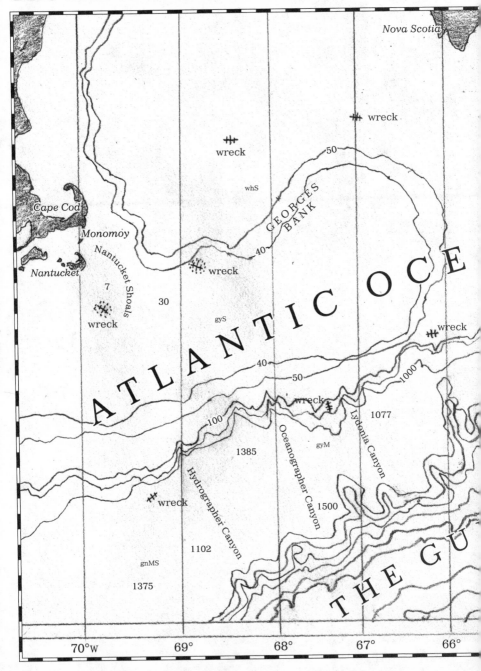

Nova Scotia

wreck

50

wreck

whS

Cape Cod

GEORGES BANK

Monomoy

40

Nantucket

Nantucket Shoals

wreck

wreck

7

30

gyS

wreck

A T L A N T I C   O C E

40

50

1000

wreck

100

1077

Lydonia Canyon

1385

Oceanographer Canyon

gyM

1500

wreck

Hydrographer Canyon

1102

gnMS

1375

T H E   G U

70°W   69°   68°   67°   66°

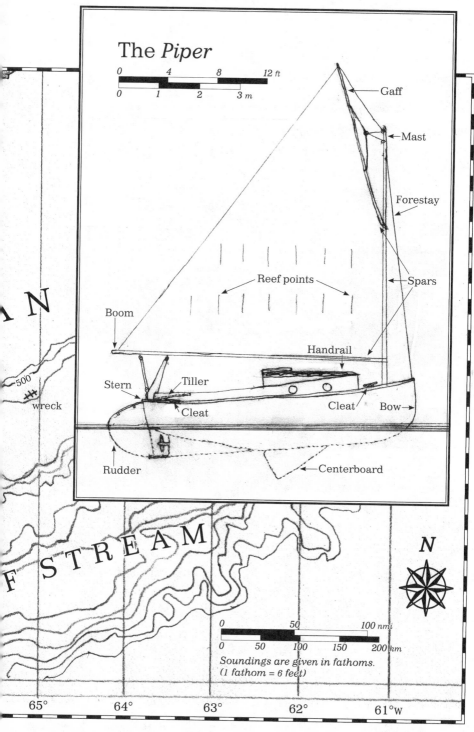

The *Piper*

0   4   8   12 ft
0   1   2   3 m

Gaff

Mast

Forestay

Reef points

Spars

Boom

Handrail

Stern

Tiller

Cleat

Cleat

Bow

Rudder

Centerboard

wreck

500

N

F STREAM

0   50   100 nmi
0   50   100   150   200 km

Soundings are given in fathoms.
(1 fathom = 6 feet)

65°   64°   63°   62°   61°w

Drawings by the author

CHAPTER ONE:
STOLEN AWAY

I should have known something weird was going on. Mom's big old leather suitcase with the broken strap was sitting in the hallway when I went into my room to finish packing. Sure, we were going on a sailing trip, and she was probably getting ready, but she would never bring along a bag as big that. There wasn't space on our little boat, and Dad wouldn't have stood for it.

I put my headphones on and jammed a few pairs of boxer shorts into my duffel bag, the last of the stuff I'd need. The CD I was listening to was my sister Beth's—a country folk band called Port Fortune she'd heard at college. I was trying to get my fill of it because I wasn't bringing any music along. Last trip we took, a leak had found its way into Beth's stuff and the saltwater made toast of her CDs and CD player. "Maybe Dad's right," she had said. "Who needs to take extra junk along when you sail?" But I could tell she was steamed.

My favorite song on the Port Fortune album was a solo sung by a guy with a voice like broken gears accompanying himself on 12-string guitar. It was fast and driving and it made me want to get up and go. It was called "Thief" and it went: *I heard you left / Gone to a foreign sea / If love is theft / You stole everything from me.*

I was listening to it for about the hundredth time when I saw our yellow Lab Mel—who was curled up on my comforter on the floor where I'd thrown it so he'd stop climbing onto my bed—lift his head and cock his ears. He must have heard something, and I thought I heard a sound, so I took my headphones off.

"Luke?"

It was my mom, outside my door.

"Yeah?"

"Could you come downstairs for a minute? I need to talk to you. And bring my suitcase down, please."

I sat up. Her voice didn't sound right. It had an edge to it. Something strange was happening. And I was already feeling strange enough as it was.

I really didn't want to go sailing with Mom and Dad, but it was something we'd been doing for years—taking a two-week cruise every summer in our cramped catboat. Every summer, that is, except for last summer, when Dad was down freelancing in New York City most of the time. It had been fun when I was a kid. But at sixteen? I had better things to do, like fishing with Chet. And this time, Beth had managed to escape to Italy.

At least when she was along we had some laughs.

Mel barged ahead of me as I hefted the bag down the stairs. He ran out the front door. I followed him onto the porch.

Out in the driveway, I saw the back of our old Defender packed with Mom's art gear. Mom crouched down when Mel ran up to her, and she held his face in her hands. His tail windmilled and he licked her face. Mom was wearing old khakis, a blue jean shirt, and tattered silk scarf—the stuff she always wore to paint in.

Dad was standing beside the truck, his hands plunged into the pockets of his madras shorts, the ones that made me cringe. He was looking at Mom as if he were trying to remember her name.

Mom stood up. "Put that in the back for me, please, Luke," she said, her voice tight, as if she couldn't move her jaw.

She came over to the truck with me. Dad stepped aside.

"What's going on?" I said.

Mom didn't say anything at first. I shoved the suitcase in the back.

"I've . . ." she said, looking down. "I've got to go away for a while."

She sighed and looked back at me. She seemed to

soften. "But I need you to take care of things. I might be gone for some time."

She took me by the shoulders and looked up at me.

"Did you grow again?" she said, smiling. Her eyes were red-rimmed and watery. Her clothes smelled of oil paint.

"Going where?" I said. This felt like one of those dreams where everything seems real but nothing's quite right.

"To Maine," she said. "To stay with my sister. I just . . . I'm sorry, Luke. If I'd known I was leaving I would have told you. This just came up. I'm sorry it's so sudden, springing this on you."

I looked at Dad. Fog slithered through the bony trunks of the locust trees. He was staring straight ahead, as if he saw something through the trees. I saw his jaw muscle working.

"Dad?" I said. "What's going on?"

He looked at me. He opened his mouth. No words came out.

"I don't get it," I said, looking back at Mom. "Why are you leaving?"

She let out a long breath.

"I just . . . I can't say. I mean I can't tell you. Not right now. But I have to go away."

"Not right now? When?" I said. "When are you coming back? What about sailing?"

She reached her hand out and touched my chin with the tips of her paint-spattered fingers.

"I'm not sure, Luke. But I'll write. Or call. I'll let you know. I'll reach you somehow."

She gave me a quick, crushing hug, walked around the truck, climbed in, slammed the door, and started the engine. Mel whined and ran toward her.

"Come here, boy," I called, and he trotted back to me, his ears laid back and his head down.

She drove off, the tires crackling over the crushed shells of the driveway. She didn't even brake when she turned onto the road. Dad and I stood there. Mel leaned against my leg. I heard the truck shift gears. Then I couldn't hear it anymore.

Dad went back into the house without a word. Mel followed him. I stood in the driveway, thinking, Is this some kind of joke? What the hell are they doing to me? Don't they know it's almost the end of summer vacation? Are they going to ruin it now?

I drifted back into the house, so confused my mouth must have been working like a fish's.

Dad was sitting in his chair in the living room. Mel pushed his face into his lap and Dad began scratching his fur.

"Dad," I said, standing in the doorway. "What did she mean? What's going on?"

"Come here a sec," he said.

I went in and stood by the window. Outside, the fog was erasing the trees.

"It means she's flown the coop," he said. He had a choked sound to his voice even though he was trying to joke. "She's going to your Aunt Lucy's place, at least for a while. I guess I didn't think she'd do it."

"Didn't think she'd do what?"

"Leave," he said. "Leave us."

"Why?" I managed to say. "Why's she leaving?"

He closed his eyes and shook his head.

"Sick of it all, I guess," he said. When he opened his eyes, I could see they were shiny. "Sick of me. Sick of all this." He flicked his hand to indicate the house.

Sick of me? I thought. Why would she be sick of me?

"Did you know she was going to leave?" I said. "Why didn't anyone tell me? When's she coming back?"

"She told me just now. Minutes before you. She said she needed to get away. For a long time. Said she needs to think things over."

He sighed. "Now that it's happened, it's . . . it's harder . . ."

It sprang out of me before I could stop it.

"What did you do?" I said. "Did you do something to her?"

He slid his eyes away from mine and stopped

scratching Mel. Mel pulled his head away and ducked out the door.

"Listen, Luke," he said, looking back at me. "She's been in her studio and hardly said a word to me for a couple of weeks. I've said nothing to her, done nothing but let her go about her business, tried not to get in her way if that's what she wants."

"But she's always in her studio."

He closed his eyes again.

"Painting there. Now she's been sleeping there, too."

I hadn't noticed. To me, Mom was painting all the time. I knew she had a cot in her studio, but I never thought about where she slept.

"I wish . . ." he said, almost whispering. "I wish I had it to do all over again. I wish I hadn't . . ." He ran his hand over his mouth and squeezed his cheeks as if to make the words come out.

I didn't get it.

"Why's she going there?" I said. "To Maine?"

He was looking out the window.

"I don't know," he said. "But I bet the Wicked Witch of Downeast put her up to it."

Whenever he mentioned Aunt Lucy, which wasn't often, that's what he called her. It was a lousy pun, if you asked me. I'd met her only once, when I was eight or nine, when we took a trip to Little Spruce Harbor, the island where she lived. I remembered her booming laugh, frizzy black hair, tie-dyed skirt, knee-high black rubber fishing boots, and not much else.

Above our fireplace hung one of the quilts she'd made. It was wild—all abstract shapes colored blue, rust, sand, and green like the seacoast. It had been hanging on that wall for as long as I could remember.

On the mantel below it stood a few framed watercolors: Dad's boat, Mom's terns, Beth's clouds, and my Mel. We always had sketchbooks, and we were always pulling them out of some pocket or backpack or satchel or handbag and sketching or painting in them. That was the way we were. Every time something grabbed me, I wanted to draw it. It made it a part of me.

Another one of the watercolors on the mantel was Mom's. It showed Dad and me goofing around on the foredeck of our boat, *Piper*. She did it last October when we were hauling the boat out for the winter. I was already as tall as him and I had him in a headlock. He was bent over, laughing hard, his sandy hair mussed up and his eyes squeezed shut, and I was staring straight at Mom, pretending to be fierce. You could barely see my face for my floppy black mop of hair.

I looked back at Dad. He wasn't looking at me. He closed his eyes again. He let out a long breath, opened his eyes slowly, and stared in silence at the gray windows.

"What are we going to do?" I said at last.

His eyes met mine.

"This looks like pretty much it," he said, giving me a brief smile before he looked away at the window again.

Maybe we wouldn't go sailing after all. I could go fishing with Chet again. Maybe I'd even call Ginnie.

"But we'll think of something," he said. "Maybe she just needs some time away. People change, right?"

"I guess," I said, feeling like I was choking.

"Look, you still want to go out to dinner? I mean, just because she changed her plans doesn't mean we have to, does it? The last thing I want to do is cook."

"I'm not that hungry," I said.

"Neither am I," he said. "But I wouldn't mind getting the hell out of here for a while. I can't sit here mooning around all night, thinking about your mother. You ready?"

"I guess so," I said. Which I wasn't. I really wanted to go back up to my room and listen to "Thief" over and over and forget about what was going on—that Mom had been stolen away, if only by herself.

We took the jeep to The Landing, a place that overlooked a harbor if you could have seen it for the fog. The harbor lights glowed as if they were underwater. The restaurant was packed with tourists and we had to take a table in the bar.

Thinking of Mom on Little Spruce Island left me dazed. It didn't make sense to me.

"So, here we are," Dad said over the noise of the restaurant.

The waitress brought him a gin and tonic and he took a quick sip. He smacked his lips and set the sweaty glass down on the napkin.

"I don't get it, Dad," I said. "People don't just do that. Why would she do it?"

"Do what?" he said.

"Take off."

He shook his head.

"You're going to have to find out from her."

"But why don't you do something?"

"Like what?" he said. "Shackle her and throw her in the brig? She does what she wants. You know that, don't you? If the spirit moves her, she goes."

He took another sip of his drink and set his glass down.

"I've made a decision," he said.

I looked at him. He was looking directly at me.

"We're going sailing anyway, just as we planned," he said. "Why shouldn't we? We'll be two castaways, sailing off to adventure, like two Sindbads. What do you think?"

I squinted at him, then looked away. I didn't know what to say. The truth was that I didn't want to go. Not now. All I could do was shrug and pick up a fried clam off my plate.

"Don't shrug," he said, his grin fading.

I wanted to shrug again, but I decided against it.

"I don't know," I said.

"You don't know what?"

"I don't know what I think about it. It's okay, I guess. But it won't be the same. Without Mom, I mean. And Beth."

"I know, I know," he said, brushing his hair out of his face. "It's okay, you guess, but you'd rather be home with your pals, right, instead of stuck out on the water with your old man? It's okay, you guess, but it won't be the same without your Mom along, right? Without Beth, who's off spending all my money in Europe?"

I didn't want him getting mad. What I wanted was to break free. That was all I wanted. Freedom. The Big Freedom to do what I wanted. When we were younger, Chet and I had talked about taking off to Wyoming to work on a ranch. "It'd be great," Chet said. "We could hitchhike out there and do whatever we wanted." I pictured Wyoming with the Grand Tetons raking saw-toothed into the blue sky and I got a kind of tickle in my stomach that made me crave to go. We would leave Harwich Port and never look back.

I craved the Big Freedom more than ever. I just didn't know where to find it.

Maybe that was what happened to Mom. Maybe she'd been fighting the urge to go for a long time. Maybe it built up until she couldn't stand it and instead of chopping Dad into chunks and throwing them in Skinequit Pond or burning the house down, she loaded up her painting stuff and bolted. But would she ever look back?

"I don't really care," I said, lying to him just so he wouldn't get angrier. "I'll go if you want to go."

He took a sip of his drink, looking at me over the rim of his glass. His eyes brightened.

"Okay, then," he said, licking his lips. "I know you don't mean it, but we might as well. The boat's ready to go. We're all packed. So it's settled. We'll shove off tomorrow, just as we planned."

But Mom had changed the plans. And now nothing felt right.

We said nothing on our ride home. The house stood like a black hulk when we crackled up the driveway and put the jeep in the garage. We'd forgotten to leave a light on. Even when Mom was immersed in a painting, rushing to get canvases ready for a show, or just shuffling around, looking out the windows, working out an idea, if I came home after dark, I'd always glance up to see her studio lights burning.

"Mel?" I said when I walked in the hallway and flipped on the light. "Where are you, boy?"

Usually he was right there to greet you. I called him again and went to the foot of the stairs. I heard the scuffle of toenails and paws and then he rattled down. Dad came around the corner just as Mel bounded down the last three steps and shouldered into his legs, driving him against the door frame, before veering into the living room.

"Settle down!" shouted Dad as Mel galloped through the living room, holding himself low to the ground. He swung his hindquarters around and came to a halt in the middle of the room, his rump raised and his paws extended before him. His ears were twisted and he was panting.

"He must have been hiding in Mom's studio," I said as Dad took a step toward him. "He's all wound up."

"I told you to SETTLE DOWN," yelled Dad again as he advanced toward Mel. Mel sprang off across the rug and rocketed past Dad and me, tore down the hall, banged into something, and came charging back in to brush past Dad.

Dad grabbed his right ear and tweaked it and yelled, "No, Mel! I told you to SETTLE DOWN. Bad dog!"

Mel shrieked and rolled over on his side and flailed his legs.

"What the hell did you do that for?" I screamed. I found myself standing next to him. "You're sick, you know that? What the hell did you have to hurt him for?"

"You, you," said Dad, rising up. His face flared red. Through clenched jaws he hissed, "You shut your mouth."

"You shut *your* mouth!" I screamed so loud my voice cracked. I realized that I was looking down at him. At that moment I thought I was going to hit him as hard as I could, hit him square on the nose so I could hear the cartilage crunch and make his selfish smile vanish. But instead I spun around and snatched the picture of the two of us off the mantel and pivoted and hurled it like a discus at the quilt. The frame and glass smashed, shards showered to the floor and a piece of the frame flew to the floor, almost hitting Mel. Mel flinched, jumped up, and scrambled out of the room. I wanted to grab the quilt and yank it down and rip it into tatters, but instead I turned, stomped out, and banged up the stairs to my room. I slammed the door and threw myself on my bed. I had no tears. My heart throbbed in my throat. I punched my headboard, a feeble punch, luckily, given that I was lying down, but the pain in my fist brought me around. I lay face down on my pillow as I gradually calmed down.

Later that night I heard a tap at the door, and I heard Dad say, "Luke, it's okay," but I said nothing. I waited for a long time, and then I tiptoed out to hunt for Mel. I found him in Mom's dark studio, curled up under the cot. I had to give him three treats before I could coax him back to my room.

CHAPTER TWO:
MORNING TIDE

Every few minutes I checked the clock. Then I'd roll over and chase images of picture frames smashing and Labs shrieking and Defenders turning out of the driveway. Finally I glanced at the clock again: three seventeen. Two minutes since I last looked. Two minutes of wondering why Mom left and why I blew up.

Mom. I never thought about her as much as I had in the few hours since she left. She'd always been there, gone for long stretches in her studio or to a show at a gallery, but always a presence. Most evenings, she'd reappear to cook us pasta or chicken or fish. Sometimes in the summer she made lobster rolls. She always boiled the lobsters herself, picked the meat, and toasted hotdog buns slathered in butter on the grill outside. She never added mayonnaise, saying that lobster meat was rich enough as it was. We'd eat them in the locust grove overlooking the water.

I blinked in the darkness, almost smelling the singe of the buns, and it struck me that she was the one who'd thrown the baseball with me when I was a kid. Once I'd lobbed her a pop-up and she lost it in the sun. It made a thump as it hit the crown of her head and her knees buckled. She crumpled to the coarse grass. I ran to her, the thought that I'd hurt her—or even killed her—devouring me. When I got to her she was rubbing her head and laughing.

"Should've had it," she said.

A solo cricket chirped close by, and the water down at the cove lapped at the beach. A whiff of coffee reached me.

That's it, I thought. Might as well get up.

I reached over to shut off the alarm, kicked off the sheets, and slid out of bed. I threw on my khaki shorts, a T-shirt, and a sweatshirt.

I walked down the hall to the bathroom and flicked on the light. My eyes were bleary in the toothpaste-spattered mirror. Maybe now would be a good time to hack off all my hair—make myself look like a convict heading onto a prison ship. But I'd probably only end up looking like I'd had an accident with a lawn mower. I stroked the sparse stubble on my upper lip and decided that shaving could wait. So I tugged a brush through my mop, splashed cold water on my face and toweled myself off, then switched off the light and went downstairs.

In the kitchen, Dad was sitting at the table, a mug of steaming black coffee in front of him.

He was already dressed in his sailing garb: an ancient white polo shirt with the peeling alligator emblem and the rumpled collar turned up, khaki shorts (thank God they weren't those funky madras shorts, but I was sure he'd packed them) that were frayed around the hem, gray socks slouched down around his ankles, and scuffed-up moccasins. He had his moth-eaten blue-and-white sweater slung around his neck. His hazel eyes were filmy and more bloodshot than mine, his hair tousled.

"There's my first mate," he said, yawning. "Grab yourself a mug and let's get going so we can catch the morning tide."

Mel stutter-stepped to me, his toenails clicking on the wood floor. He curled around me, bowing his head and grinning.

I patted him and poured myself a half a mug of coffee.

Dad smiled at me. "You excited, Luke?"

I kept my eyes on my mug. I didn't want to bring up last night. Maybe I could just avoid it.

"Luke," Dad said again.

"Sure," I managed. I sipped at my mug of coffee and scratched Mel behind the ear.

Dad watched me, his eyes slightly narrowed. Maybe he didn't believe me when I said I was excited. And why should he? I wasn't.

When my mom looked at you, you knew you were

being looked at. She read your face with her eyes. She had clear, warm caramel-colored eyes that fixed on yours and drew you in. My eyes were the same color and we had the same thick black hair.

"When I paint your eyes," she said one time while I was sitting for her in her studio, "I paint my eyes."

"Just think," said Dad. "We're going to sea like the Owl and the Pussycat." He chuckled. "Did you pack your runcible spoon?"

Mel thumped his tail against my leg. Maybe he thought Dad was funny. I sure didn't.

Dad took a big breath, held it for a moment, and exhaled.

"About last night," he said.

"Ready to go when you are," I mumbled, digging my fingers into the fur beneath Mel's ear.

"Look, Luke," he said. "I wanted to tell you I'm sorry. It was just . . . I was wrong to yell at Mel. Stupid. I don't blame you for what you did. With your mother taking off and all . . ."

I kept my eyes on my mug.

"Don't worry about it," I said.

"I am worried about it. We can't let everything fall apart. But I hope . . ." He took another deep breath. ". . . I hope you can forgive me."

I didn't say anything. My insides were twisting. All

this emotion was embarrassing. Everything was falling apart. Who was he trying to kid?

Maybe that was why Mom had taken off: so she wouldn't have to go on this sailing trip with Dad.

He stood up and set his mug in the sink. "You hungry? I can fix you something before we go."

"No," I said. "No, thanks."

"Okay," he said. "Then why don't you bring the jeep around. Want to drive us to the harbor?"

I had my learner's permit and I almost said yes. But if I drove, Dad would give me pointers. I felt like hiding. I wanted to stay silent.

"That's okay," I said. "You can drive."

He washed out his mug and set it on the counter to dry. Then he grinned at me.

"Well, why don't you finish getting ready so we can get a move on, buddy," he said. "This is going to be a great trip. In spite of everything."

When I passed the living room on my way upstairs, I saw that Dad had cleaned up the broken glass. The painting, no longer in a frame, was set up on the mantel in its same old spot. The quilt still hung on the wall. A scratch zigzagged across it.

We packed the last of the gear into the jeep, saving just enough room in the back seat for Mel. Then we drove over to Chet's house, where Mel would stay during our trip.

We bumped onto Chet's rutted sand driveway and parked the jeep. Mel leaped out when he spotted Poppy, Chet's three-legged Welsh corgi mix, hobbling toward us through the overgrown lawn. They tore off to horse around among the old skiffs and broken engine parts and long tufts of grass in the backyard.

"Don't be long," said Dad. "I don't want to miss that tide."

Chet was drinking coffee at the kitchen table, wearing a pair of ripped jeans and no shirt. The kitchen light was so bright it made me squint.

"Hey," I said. "I put Mel's food and stuff on the porch. I thought you were heading out to pull the traps today."

He slurped at his coffee.

"Nope. Going to New Bedford for some gear."

He took another sip.

"You're lucky," he said. "I'll be slaving away, hauling traps and fighting with the old man. He said we're sticking with sea bass because of the price."

"That's not so bad," I said. I'd gone on a few offshore trips with them and liked it a lot better than other after-school and summer jobs I'd had—working at a lobster pound, mowing lawns, tagging after a locksmith. I liked it a lot better than all the time after school I'd spent over the winter and spring helping him and his dad refurbish the boat. It was my "work/study" program with Chet, but Chet had all the know-how. All I did then was stand around freezing, listening to him bicker with his dad, Bill, about the best way to approach things. At least it got me out of school early.

"If we could go tuna fishing," he said, "I'd like it a lot more. Offshore is the best."

"That would be great."

"But you get to go sailing. Doing nothing. Catching a tan. *That's* not all bad. Even if it is with your parents."

"Ah, you know what?" I said. "It's just going to be Dad."

"Huh?"

"Mom . . . Mom left."

He looked at me through the thick lenses of his glasses.

"What do you mean?"

"She took off. To Maine. For good, I guess."

"Why?"

"I don't know," I said.

He blinked.

"That's different," he said. "Want a cup of coffee?"

"No time. Dad's got his shorts in a twist to shove off."

He looked at me again. "Ginnie ever call you?"

"Nope," I said. "After what happened, it's probably over."

He took another sip of coffee.

"Hey, who knows?" he said. "Maybe we'll see you out there. Me working for Barnacle Bill on our scow and you catching rays on your yacht."

"Some yacht. I can't even stand up straight in the cabin."

I walked toward the door.

"Well, see you later," I said.

"Hey, hang on a second. I just thought of something." He got up, went into his bedroom, and came out with a small brown paper bag.

"Take these," he said. "They're the cherry bombs left over from the Fourth. The ones we made."

"Dad probably wouldn't think it's such a great idea," I chuckled, "me carrying homemade explosives aboard."

He gave me a deadpan look and blinked at me through his glasses.

"Set off a couple of these," he said, "and you'll see how high the bluebloods in the yacht clubs can jump."

I laughed and took the bag.

"Remember blowing up the paint can?" I said.

"Our first successful spaceflight," he said. "Must have gone twenty feet straight up."

Two quick bleats of the jeep horn sounded outside.

"Better get going."

"Okay," he said, getting up to pour himself more

coffee. "See you later." I stuffed the paper bag deep into my shorts pocket and went out the door.

When we got to the end of Chet's driveway, Dad said, "Let's take a quick drive down to Red River Beach to see what the water's like." I had thought he wanted to get to the boat right away to catch the tide. Maybe he was stalling after all.

The beach parking lot was empty. He stopped at the end by the jetty and climbed up on the hood for a better view.

Nantucket Sound spread out before us dark and quiet. The stars sprawled overhead even as dawn showed a hint of blue along the eastern horizon.

One evening back in the springtime, I was walking home with Ginnie Dahl. We'd been hanging out at the benches in Harwich Port. She was on foot, and I was walking my bike, the bike making its ticking sound as we ambled along.

"Let's go down to Red River," she said. "It's still early."

Dusk had fallen by the time we got to the beach. We walked down to the jetty, right where we were parked now.

"Cool," she said, looking up at the sky. "I've never seen so many stars." We picked our way over the boulders of the jetty and sat down together on the smoothest one we could find at the end. Just below our feet, small waves snuffled at the rocks.

"Look out there," I said. "You can see all the way to Nantucket. That's Great Point Light."

She shivered. "Kind of chilly."

I glanced at her and inched closer so that our shoulders were pressed tight together.

Maybe I should put my arm around her, I thought. It felt good to be so close.

"You can put your arm around me," she said. Then she chuckled. "I won't bite it off."

So I brought my arm up and around her shoulders and drew her closer. She rested her head against my chest. Her hair smelled like a cool flower.

We both saw it at the same time. The shooting star came out of the sky above the sea in a long bright arc. It split in two, and the two streaks split again, and then all the glowing trails dissolved in silence above the water.

I felt her exhale and nudge closer within the circle of my arm.

At last she whispered, "I've never seen anything like that."

"Flat as a millpond," announced Dad from the jeep hood. He jumped down and got back in. "Looks like we'll be motoring for a while. But the tide's still headed out so we'll have it with us for a while."

Before we left the house, I was too tired and keyed up to eat, but now that we were bouncing back up Deep Hole Road to Main Street, the cool air whipping in the open jeep, my stomach growled. Even one of Ginnie's blueberry muffins would be good right now. Well, then again, maybe not.

I'd been riding my bike to school one drizzly morning when Ginnie called me on my cell phone.

"Meet me at the ballfield before school," she said. "I have something for you."

She was already waiting for me in the dugout when I arrived. Water droplets beaded up on the roof and dripped onto the wooden steps. I sat beside her on the bench.

"I made these for you last night," she said, pulling a paper bag out of her backpack. "Want one?"

She handed it to me. It felt like a bag of rocks. I peered inside. Three giant blueberry muffins huddled together. I had already eaten a bowl of oatmeal and two slices of toast. I didn't have room for a blueberry boulder.

But I hauled one out.

"Looks great," I said.

She smiled. Her cheeks were wet from the drizzle and rosy from the chill.

I knew what I had to do. I peeled off the paper and took a bite.

The chewing went okay at first, and I nodded at Ginnie to show how good it was. But maybe I'd bitten off too much. My mouth was full of something like wet cement. The more I chewed, the more my throat constricted.

But the happiness in her green eyes made me choke down a clot of it.

"What do you think?" she said, looking at me hopefully. "Too dense?"

"No, excellent," I said, still chewing. "Make these yourself?"

When I saw her eyes light up, I forced myself to take another bite.

The harbor parking lot was empty except for a few fishermen's pickup trucks sitting by the row of shanties. We parked the jeep on the dock, then crossed the shell-littered beach, threads of cobwebs lacing my face, to launch the dinghy. We rowed across the still water of the harbor, climbed aboard *Piper*, got the motor cranked up, and headed back in.

I finished tying up and Dad shut off the engine. The morning quiet returned. No one else was around except a gull that stood on one of the far pilings, mewing and chuckling. The harbor water spread out slick as mercury.

All the boats rested at their moorings in silence. Across the harbor, gulls facing the same way roosted on the roof peak of the Boat Works building. Mom would have said that it was an Edward Hopper moment—the gray and white gulls facing the same way against the dark blue sky, the graying light stark and pure.

Six years before, we'd first launched *Piper* at this same harbor on a June evening when the no-see-ums were swarming. She had been built in 1931—a 22-foot Herbert F. Crosby catboat. "Looks like the one in *Ground Swell*," Mom had said, "one of my favorite Hoppers." The boat needed to be rebuilt from the ground up. Dad hired a man named Alden Eastman to do the work. Alden Eastman even made some changes to the original design, like adding a quarterberth beneath the cockpit, an engine hatch in the companion-way bulkhead, and a chart table in the cabin. It took him over a year to finish.

Mom, Beth, and I stood around by the Boat Works launch ramp swatting bugs as the boat, which had been the *Miss Martha*, now rechristened *Piper*, splashed off the trailer. Dad was aboard to throw a line to Alden Eastman. I remembered Alden Eastman gazing at *Piper* bobbing bright and high-prowed at the dock. He took off his sweat-stained green work cap and scratched the top of his bald head. In a soft tone, he said to Dad,

"She's riding fine, just fine, and pretty as a feather." I jumped aboard and stood next to Dad. He put his arm around me and said, "She's finally in the water, buddy. Isn't she beautiful?"

In the first month, Dad made about twenty water-colors of her, and it seemed our family was on the boat that whole summer, making day trips, cruising on weekends. Sometimes Dad and I even went down to the harbor just to sleep overnight on her. Mom made a huge oil of her that she sold to someone on the dock before she had even finished.

"That looks like just about it," said Dad after we'd stowed most of the gear. "Do me a favor and get the rest put away, would you? I have a quick errand to run."

"Sure thing."

I went below. When I pulled the bag of firecrackers out of my pocket to stuff them in my seabag, I found my cell phone in there, too. I meant to leave it at home. Stupid. Cell phones didn't mix with saltwater any better than CDs. But I didn't want to leave it in the jeep, either.

For a moment, I thought that since I had my phone, I might as well call Ginnie. But instead I found a bag-gie in one of the galley drawers, dropped the phone in, sealed it up, and stuffed it in the bottom of my seabag along with the firecrackers.

This trip, my berth was the one that Mom slept in opposite Dad's. It was an upgrade from my usual spot on an air mattress on the cabin deck or, when the weather was good, on one of the cockpit seats.

Beth slept in the quarterberth, and at first I'd thought I might sleep there, but we'd stowed a bunch of gear on it. I liked the quarterberth. It was aft of the main cabin, beneath the cockpit, a cramped but secret hiding place. The first year we had *Piper*, Beth and I sometimes wedged ourselves in there and played Fish or Crazy Eights. It was like a clubhouse.

I came back topside and looked out over the harbor. A pair of sanderlings swerved above the water, then swooped in for a landing on the far slice of beach. A fish broke the surface just beyond *Piper*. A bat fluttered above the dock.

I glanced below at the rest of the gear. I'd have to climb back down there and shove it around, manhandle it into lockers and racks or dump in on the quarterberth.

Screw it, I thought. I'll get to it later.

I sat down on the cockpit seat to watch the morning, and I wondered what Ginnie would say if she were sitting beside me. It was strange. Sometimes she said things that made me think she understood me. But other times, especially the spring evening on Bank Street Beach, what she said made me want to disappear.

We'd been sitting in silence, watching the sky turn peach, when she said, "I saw one of your drawings in the art show yesterday, the one of the boat." She paused. A gull flew past and let out a long whine. Then she said quietly, "It was the best in the school."

I didn't know what to say. If you lived in a family like mine, you knew that no drawing or painting you did was going to be the best one. Someone was always making something better. It didn't matter that the drawing, a sketch of a yawl moored in Wychmere Harbor, won first prize. I didn't even show it to Mom or Dad when I took it home.

But I said, "Thanks."

She had her arms wrapped around her knees. The cuffs of her jeans were rolled up. She dug one bare foot in the cold sand and looked at me.

"Would you draw me?" she said. "I'd really like you to."

I glanced at her. The light was on her cheek and in her green eyes and copper hair.

Why her question made me feel as though I'd been invaded I wasn't sure. I should have taken it as a compliment but it felt like she wanted something from me. I felt something go cool inside me.

Still, I wasn't about to tell her that. So I said, "Sure. If you want me to."

But I couldn't shake that feeling. Whenever I was

with her—even taking a walk with her on the beach—
I felt crowded. I got tongue-tied, thinking that the question was going to crop up again. It never did, but it hung between us.

It was the week before Mom left, and I was in my room. I was listening to that CD of Beth's while I was sketching Mel, who was snoring on my comforter on the floor.

My cell phone rang, and I saw Ginnie's number light up. Mel snorted, lifted his head, cocked an ear, then dropped his head back down and sighed.

I let it ring. Part of me wanted to talk to her, but part of me didn't. I let it ring till it stopped.

I went back to drawing Mel for a while, but then the part of me that wanted to talk to her came on strong. So I put my pencil and sketchbook down and called.

"Hey," I said. "What's up?"

"Not much," she said. "You busy?"

"Not really," I said, and then I let it slip out before I could stop it. "Just sketching Mel."

She was silent. I could guess what she was thinking: You have time to draw your old dog, but not me.

She didn't say anything, though, but even imagining what she was thinking made me mad. It was as though she felt she owned me.

"You know that sailing trip I told you about?" I said. "We're leaving next week."

She didn't say anything.

"So I guess it's going to be hard to hang out together," I said, "Dad said there's a lot we have to do to get ready."

Now I was lying. Dad had never said such a thing.

"But maybe," I said, "I can, you know, give you a call, if I get free or something. Or you can call me."

She wasn't making this easy.

"Ginnie?" I said. "You still there?"

I heard her exhale. "So that's the way it's going to be," she said. Then, in a low, cold tone I hadn't heard from her before, she said, "Have fun," and hung up.

Mel cracked open an eye when I put the phone down on my bedside table. I sat back against my pillow and stared at the windows. Nothing felt right. Maybe all along I wanted to like her more than I really did. But I didn't know why I couldn't get myself to open up to her.

It took me a while to get back to my sketch of Mel. You can't draw right when you feel like a coward.

I looked out at the harbor, and I pictured Ginnie picking her way barefoot along the beach. I was thinking maybe I should dig my phone out and call her when the jeep rolled back down the dock.

Dad climbed aboard, carrying a white cardboard box tied with string, a box of meltaways from Bonatt's

Bakery. They were my favorites. You had to have melt-aways fresh and warm. There was no other way to eat them. Even if you reheated them in your own oven, they didn't measure up to what they were when you first got them—all steamy and soft and light and gooey and sweet and rich with the scent of butter and almonds.

It was always Mom who brought them home for me. She liked to sit at the kitchen table, her work-hardened hands wrapped around a cup of black coffee, and watch me cut the strings, open up the top and inhale the steam, and polish off a couple. She would slice herself a small wedge and chew it slowly, relishing it.

But this time it was Dad who handed me the box. Sure, it felt the same—still warm underneath and hefty—but I knew the pastries wouldn't taste the same. Nothing was the same.

"Everything all stowed?" he said, looking around him. His brow was furrowed. He looked miffed.

"Umm, I was just about to finish," I said.

"You mean you didn't do it?"

That's exactly what I mean, I thought. What's the big deal?

"Anyway, let's finish up," he said at last. "I'm going to go park the jeep and then we'll shove off, okay?"

Tell him you're not going, a voice said inside me. Tell him you'll stay ashore with Chet. Stay home. Don't go.

But I didn't say anything.

Dad climbed back up and got two containers of coffee out of the jeep. He leaned over and handed them down to me.

"Take these," he said. "And don't eat all the meltaways before I get back."

"Aye-aye," I said.

"That's 'Aye-aye, *Sir*,'" he said as he stood up, grinning, and got into the jeep. I went below and started to shove the rest of the stuff into the lockers. I let the box sit on the galley counter. It would cool off in no time. I didn't care.

When he returned, he stood in the cockpit and surveyed the harbor. He brushed his hair off his forehead.

"If we forgot anything," he said, "it won't matter out there, will it? Want to get the bow line?"

So it was really going to happen. There was nothing I could do but go.

Dad hit the starter and the diesel grumbled to life. I climbed back on the dock, untied the lines, and jumped aboard.

We slipped away from the dock and crossed the smooth water, two silver ribbons of wake spreading out behind us. I coiled the lines and shoved them in the cockpit locker. A gull swimming in front of us spread its wings but didn't bother to take off. It bobbed on our wake as we slid past it.

We angled through the channel between the jetties and crossed the outer harbor. I went forward to stand at the bow, gripping onto the forestay. I took a few deep breaths of the rich sea air, and something seemed to lift from me. Dad revved up the motor and we swept past the channel buoys. Daylight was brightening the sky to the east. I turned around and watched the buildings and beachline and breakwater begin to recede, the thrill of heading out and leaving everything behind fluttering through my stomach.

"How about getting us a couple of those meltaways," called Dad from the tiller, "before they get stone cold?"

I went below and cut the string with a knife, lifted the lid, and couldn't stop myself from leaning down to sniff them. Their sweet warmth rose up to me.

Dad was sipping his coffee when I handed up two meltaways and stepped into the cockpit.

"This isn't all bad, is it?" he said as I sat down.

I sank my teeth into the warm pastry. I'd been wrong. It tasted as good as ever. But it wasn't the same without Mom.

Still, it was true that it wasn't all bad. The sinking feeling I'd felt before we shoved off was easing, and the smooth course of the boat soothed me. Maybe it wouldn't be so terrible after all—if I could stop thinking about Ginnie, about Mom. Maybe I'd just been hungry.

I took my coffee forward to stand at the bow. I held onto the forestay and leaned against the mast and watched the day come on. The horizon was a pencil line between the navy-blue water and the sky going greenish gold as dawn arrived. I felt a fleck of meltaway crumb on my lip and I pushed it into my mouth with my finger. Once, when I was about nine, I tiptoed into Mom's studio to show her a watercolor I'd done of the cove below the house and a flock of clouds grazing through the sky above it. I was proud of it because I thought I'd finally figured out how to do light on water.

She turned and looked at me for a moment, as if trying to figure out what kind of creature I was, then set her brush down, wiped her hands on her pants, and held them out for my painting. "Let's have a look," she said, tilting her head to the side, tipping the paper to the light. She studied it for a while and I began to get nervous, running through a list of things she could criticize. Then she nodded and said, "One thing. You need to soften the edges of the clouds. Like this." She wet the tip of her finger with her tongue and worked her finger along the clouds till the paint became gauzy. Then she held it out, tilted her head one way, then the other, and handed it back.

"There," she said, smiling gently. "It's the best one you've done, Luke."

I looked at it again and loved it more because she loved it.

Then Dad began bellowing, "Someone's in the kitchen with Dinah, someone's in the kitchen I know-O-O-O . . ." over the rumble of the engine.

I wished Mom were with me. Here she had just left, and Dad was singing to the morning. You would've thought he was glad she was gone. But I guessed that he was trying to mask how he was really feeling, which annoyed me even more.

Beautiful day or not, I was trapped with him.

CHAPTER THREE:
SEA TRIALS

We powered over the steel-slick surface of Nantucket Sound. The sun broke free of the horizon, spreading golden sheets of light across the water. The long sandy spine of Monomoy, two islands of dunes and scrub that separated the Sound from the open ocean, lay along the eastern horizon. Chet and I had gone out there a handful of times in his skiff to bodysurf in the rollers on the ocean side and fish the rips off the Point. It was a wild and spooky place with its abandoned lighthouse and history of vanished settlements.

Mom and I went out there, too, last summer when Dad was in New York. Beth drove back to Providence early, before her classes at the Rhode Island School of Design started up again, to work at her job at a frame store, "paying my dues and trying not to cut off my thumbs," as she put it.

Actually, Dad had been home once for about a week before going back to New York again, and now that I thought about it, watching the island pass to our east, Mom had vanished into her studio after he went back the second time. I didn't see her for days except when she came out to make us something to eat. Then early one morning she was in the kitchen when I came down, and she said, "We're going sailing. Get your stuff." I was leery of it at first—I'd never sailed with just her—but we got underway okay. A few cottony tufts of cloud sailed across the sky almost low enough to graze our masthead as we made the short sail over to the island, the dinghy in tow. We dropped the anchor in the shallows of Common Flats and rowed ashore. Mom brought only a small knapsack, a couple of granola bars and bananas, a canteen, and her sketchbook in it. We hiked all over, spooked a deer, watched the seals with their understanding eyes lying on the beach, listened to the screech and cheers of the gulls and terns.

"Terns are my favorites," she said, bracing her sketchbook on her left forearm. She squinted at the birds flying overhead, her right hand capturing them on the page as if under its own power. "I love their fork tails. And look at their heads. Don't they look like they're wearing black visors?"

We sat for a long time on the deserted beach, watching the rollers rumble in from the Atlantic. She made a mosaic out of the same-sized flat stones she found scattered on the sand. She worked away in silence, piecing together a perfect circle, for over two hours. When she finished, she put her hands on her hips and looked at what she'd done.

"It's a landing pad for terns," she said, chuckling.

The afternoon shadows lengthened under the High Bank, the ocean-facing dunes, and Mom said, "We should camp out here. We could bring gear from the boat." It sounded good to me—I thought of all the shooting stars we'd probably see—but then I remembered something.

"What about Mel?" I said.

"Right," she sighed. "Where's that Beth when you need her? I should have remembered to bring Mel along."

"He gets pretty antsy on the boat."

"That's true, too."

When we trekked back over the biscuit-colored dunes, she didn't say a word. She seemed to sink deeper into the gloomy side of herself as the light faded.

Watching Monomoy pass in the distance gave me an idea. I looked at Dad as he turned his face to the sun. I wondered whether he'd go for what I was thinking about. Chet would. Mom would. Beth would.

I went back aft and sat in the cockpit beside him.

"Hey, Dad," I said. "Have you ever been out to Monomoy? Gone ashore there?"

He glanced out to the east, then back at me.

"Nope. Sailed by it a couple of times. Remember going to the Point two years ago?"

I looked toward it.

"Sure," I said. "But I'm talking about landing on it. Chet and I climbed up on the lighthouse once. And you know when Mom and I went out there, when you were in New York?"

He looked at me. For a moment, his eyes lost their light.

"Yes," he said. "Your mother told me about it."

"It's weird," I said. "Kind of scary, but beautiful. Haunted or something."

"I can imagine."

I glanced at him. He checked the compass and then looked back out at Monomoy.

"Maybe we could head over there," I said. "Drop the anchor and go ashore, the way Mom and I did."

He was still looking at the island.

"I heard that there used to be a place on it called Whitewash Village," I said. "The harbor was deep enough for schooners until it filled up with sand."

"No kidding?" said Dad, looking at me.

"Anyway, what do you think?" I was getting excited about exploring the island again.

"I don't know," said Dad. "We still have a long trip to Nantucket."

I could tell that he wasn't wild about the idea. I had to be careful and not push too hard.

"Chet and I body surfed out on the Atlantic side, too," I said. "Nobody else was out there. One wave picked Chet up and dumped him on bare sand and then crashed down on him. He got a bloody nose from it and was so dazed he didn't know where he was for a few minutes."

We powered along, the throb of the engine filling our silence.

"And Mom even wanted to camp out there," I said. "Can you believe it?"

"Look," said Dad, pointing to the west, away from Monomoy. "Seems to be a breeze coming up."

"So do you want to go out there?" I said. "Out to Monomoy?"

Dad looked at me.

"It sounds like a good idea," he said. "But we should get to Nantucket first. Maybe we can head back tomorrow or some other day."

"But look at it," I said. "It's right there."

I could feel anger scratching around inside me again. Why did he get to call all the shots?

"I thought," I said, "that we were free to do what we wanted."

I saw him glance at the island. He didn't say anything.

"I don't get it," I said. "Monomoy's right there. There's nothing to be afraid of."

He shot me a look.

"I'm not afraid," he said. "But for one, the water's too shoal, and two, the tides around there are wild."

I leaned back against the bulkhead and crossed my arms. I looked away from Dad. Even the sight of him ticked me off. Besides, it wasn't me who was afraid to try something new. Mom and I had sailed there. Dad had always said that catboats with their shallow draft were made for shoal water. So what was the problem?

"Hey, the breeze is definitely starting to puff," he said. "Want to get the sail up?"

I kept my eyes on the water.

"Whatever," I said.

I felt him looking at me.

"Look, Luke," he said. "We'll go out there at some point, just as I said. We've got to get to the mooring or we'll lose our reservation. It's packed at this time of the year. We'll see what the weather's like and then head out there in a day or two, okay?"

"Awesome," I said.

"Okay, then," he said. "Let's get the sail up."

"Super," I said.

"And Luke?"

I didn't say anything.

"If you can't say anything without being sarcastic," he said, "don't say anything at all."

I got up and climbed over the cabintop to undo the sail cover. If that's what he wanted, that's what I'd give him. Silence. I was sure that if Mom were here, she'd be on my side.

I glanced back at Dad in the cockpit. He had put on the stupid hat he called his "sailing lid," a floppy khaki hat with the brim turned up in front that he had picked up at an army-navy store years before.

"You've got to be kidding me," I said under my breath. I looked around. At least no boat was close enough to see him. Maybe I could snatch it off his head and toss it to a passing gull.

"What was that?" he said.

"Nothing," I said.

"What's eating you, Luke?"

"Nothing."

"Well, stop acting like a baby. You're sixteen years old, for God's sake."

His face had turned brick red. His knuckles were white from gripping the tiller.

"You think I feel great?" he said, a fleck of spit leaping off his lips. "You think I'm having a great goddamn time? Thinking about your mother up and leaving me like I'm some sort of scum? What do you think about that? What do you think about someone else feeling lousy for a change instead of dwelling on yourself? Huh? How does THAT make you feel?"

Christ, I thought. He's flipping out. He's so mad he doesn't even know he's spitting.

I had all the ties in my fist and I pictured flinging them overboard and then diving in after them and swimming to Monomoy. I stared at him and he stared right back at me. I could see his chest rising and falling fast, and I realized that mine was doing the same.

"Damn," he said at last, his voice cracking. He sighed, closed his eyes, and shook his head. Then he looked back at me.

"This isn't going to be easy, is it?" he said. "But you've got to cut me a break, Luke. You may not want to be here, but here is where we are. Try to make the most of it. Try thinking about someone else besides yourself."

I exhaled. When I started looping the sail ties around each other, I realized my hands were shaking.

"Better get the sail up," he said.

I threw the knot of sail ties into the cabin. Now I was the one who felt like a jerk.

Just keep your mouth shut, I said to myself. But even talking to myself didn't make me feel any less hollow inside.

* * * *

The breeze rose with the sun. With the sail up, the only sounds came from the boat and the sea. I stayed silent, and so did Dad. I listened to the burble of the wake and the splash of the bow parting the water as we ran toward Nantucket. I kept my eyes on the water.

In the late morning, Nantucket appeared on the southern horizon like a mirage. Soon the island materialized, and I saw the white column of Great Point Light at the eastern point of the island. Far behind us I saw what must have been a big vessel, but we'd be in the harbor before we'd have to worry about it.

By the time we got near the bell buoy outside the harbor entrance, we had to keep an eye out for the boats cutting across our bow and overtaking us.

"Let's get the engine on," said Dad. "We'll drop the sail when we're farther inside." He radioed ahead to the mooring service for the number of the mooring.

We entered the wide channel between two long jetties. The tide was nearly high, and the rocks of the breakwater on both sides were almost covered with blue-green water.

The channel was packed with boats. When I looked at Dad, my heart sank.

"Dad," I said, "what are you going to do with that hat?"

CRAIG MOODIE

He glanced at me. "What hat?" He looked upward. "My sailing lid?"

"Yeah."

He frowned. "What about it?"

"Well," I said, forcing a laugh, "it's ridiculous."

"Ridiculous? You mean 'lid-iculous,' don't you?"

"Come on, Dad," I said. "You know it is. Want me to put it below?"

He chuckled. "You're worried what other people think?"

I looked around. Boats were everywhere.

"Not exactly. But you don't want people to think you're a geek, do you?"

He looked at me.

"What you mean is, you don't want people to think you're the geek. Maybe I should make you wear it."

"Fat chance," I said.

"Well, I'll tell you something, Luke," he said, leaning toward the starter. "I don't give a rat's ass what other people think."

"Whoa," I said. "Don't get all worked up."

"I'm not all worked up."

I thought, Maybe he'll try to twist my ear like he did to Mel. The thought almost made me snicker.

"But if it'll make you happy," he said, "I'll take the god-damn thing off." He reached up, tore it off his head, and whipped it like a boomerang into the cabin.

— 47 —

"Satisfied?" he said, brushing his hair off his forehead.

I smiled.

"Satisfied," I said.

Then he hit the starter and the engine clucked a few times and fell silent. He hit it twice more with the same result.

Behind us, the high-speed ferry, a massive black-hulled catamaran with a white cabin that looked like an ocean-going space shuttle, was rounding the entrance buoy on its way into the harbor. That was the vessel I'd seen not long before on the horizon. It had come up fast. A speedboat veered around us, its wake slapping *Piper*'s bow and spraying us with seawater. *Piper* bounded over the wake, rocking hard, then settled.

The wind picked up the closer we got to land, and now we began to surge ahead as our big sail pulled harder. We were running almost directly before the wind. A great, deep bellow of a horn blasted. Toward the inner harbor, past Brant Point Light, I saw the masts of the steamship, the big old slow ferry, moving into the channel.

"Doesn't sound good," said Dad after he tried the engine again. "Take the helm for me."

I gripped onto the tiller and looked behind me at the fast ferry looming up behind us. It could travel at forty knots or so and it hadn't slowed down yet.

Dad pulled up the hatch in the cockpit and peered

down at the silent engine. He brushed his hair off his forehead. I looked behind us again.

Dad closed the hatch and jumped below. He flung open the toolbox and began clanging and clanking through it.

The ferry closed down on us, looking as big as an aircraft carrier, its turbine engines roaring.

What was I doing at the helm? I'd never sailed in such close quarters before. What was he trying to prove?

"Dad," I said.

Now a Friendship sloop about thirty feet long was tacking out of the channel. She was a beauty of a boat, all glossy white paint and gaff-rigged like us, though she had twin headsails. She must have been some sort of party boat. Her cockpit, decks, and cabintop were crowded with people. She had just come about and was close-hauled and headed dead for us.

Now, hulking around Brant Point, the steamship swung into the channel.

"Dad," I said again, louder this time.

More rummaging sounds came from below.

The fast ferry was only about fifty yards behind us. The sloop was cutting across the channel in front of the ferry, on a collision course for us.

"Dad!" I called. My palms were sweating. My vision went hazy.

"What?" he said. "Where's that can of ether? Do you remember where I put it?"

"Dad, we've got to do something here." I had trouble making my tongue work.

At last the jetlike whine of the fast ferry's engine subsided as the vessel throttled down to idle into the main part of the channel. It was now so close off our port stern that I could have hit it with a seashell.

The sloop was clear of the ferry's bow but she continued on a beeline for us. She was on the starboard tack, meaning she had the right of way.

"Dad," I yelled. "We've got to come about or something."

"What?" he said.

With the three-story cliffside of the ferry passing to port, the only thing I could do was haul the tiller toward me. We swung away from the heeling sloop. Turning the boat around to the other tack flung the boom around on the other side in an uncontrolled jibe. Boom and sail slammed around with a crack and a bang. I didn't duck fast enough and the mainsheet flogged me across the neck and cheek and knocked me to the cockpit rail. Red and blue and green lights needled through my eyes. For a moment, I thought I was looking down the wrong end of a pair of binoculars. The boat lunged as the wind filled the sail.

"What happened?" said Dad as he tumbled back topside, holding the can of ether.

I got up and grabbed the tiller again. We heeled and yawed over the ferry's wake.

"Bring her around," he growled. "We're headed for the rocks."

The sloop came about again at the point where we'd been heading and cut back across the channel behind the fast ferry. The steamship was lumbering past the fast ferry and blew its horn so long and hard that I felt vibrations in the soles of my feet. We bounded over its steep wake. Skiffs and fishing boats and sailboats worked their way in and out of the channel.

The sloop swept past our port side with only a few yards to spare. I could hear the skipper say, "Let's get that jib sheet in tighter." I spotted a girl working the lines in the cockpit. She was tailing for a guy cranking a winch, hauling back on the line as hard as she could. The other people sitting around were doing nothing, smiles plastered on their faces. She was tan and wore her honey-colored hair in a ponytail that stuck out the back of her Red Sox cap. She looked at me, gave me a big grin, and waved back and forth with her whole tan arm while she held the line with one hand. I wanted to dive for the cockpit floor, feeling stupid for screwing up. The rope burns on my cheek throbbed. I gave her a quick wave in return.

The other people aboard waved back at me, almost in unison. I would have been amused if I hadn't been so embarrassed.

As the boat passed us, I saw that the nameboard read *Endeavor.*

"Luke, for God's sake," cried Dad. He grabbed the tiller and shouted, "Ready about, hard alee!" and *Piper's* bow swung past the rocks as we came about. I glanced over the side to see a row of rocks draped with yellow and green weed and algae just below the surface. We missed them by inches.

"Luke, tighten that mainsheet," said Dad, his voice strained. "We have to come about again."

I glanced at him. His lips were clamped down in a white line and his jaw muscles flexed.

Now we were headed the wrong way—back out of the channel.

"I can't believe this," said Dad. "The engine craps out on us and then you almost put us on the rocks."

I shot him a look as I gripped the sheet. I gave it a mighty pull as he pointed the bow as close to the wind as possible.

"Tighter," he said.

Anger surged through me and I yanked at the line again.

"Okay, ready about," he said, looking behind him

at two sailboats powering out of the channel. The fast ferry was rounding Brant Point by now and the steamship had cleared the breakwaters, headed into the Sound.

We came about, bringing the boat back in the right direction. When I eased the sheet, Dad told me to take the helm again. He tried the engine. This time it started up and purred away as if nothing had ever been wrong.

"Can you believe it?" he said, his face now relaxing. "This thing's always been fluky. I'll take the helm now if you want."

"I didn't want it in the first goddamn place," I said before I could stop myself. I saw him raise his eyebrows as I climbed out of the cockpit. I stomped forward to stand at the bow. I gripped onto the forestay and kept my eyes on the passing boats and the harbor coming into view. My cheeks were burning. The last thing I wanted to see at that moment was my old man, smiling and wanting to smooth over everything.

My anger subsided as we picked our way through the moored boats, many of them tremendous megayachts and motorsailers and junior ships. They shined and gleamed and rose high above us, the small chop in the harbor splashing against their hulls. Some of them had tenders or inflatables that were bigger than *Piper*. We threaded our way through them, searching for our mooring, overshadowed by their towering hulls.

I stood at the bow with the boathook. A sickening feeling that the engine was going to conk out at the critical moment—when we were closing on the mooring and we would drift into some spotless behemoth yacht—trickled into my stomach. Dad had left the sail up just in case. He throttled back as we worked our way through the alleyways between the boats to the outer fringe of the mooring field. The boats got smaller and less showy the farther we went. The engine had made a fool of me before, and I was sure it would try to again.

"There's our mooring," I called to Dad. "38 OT dead ahead."

"Got it," he said, swinging the bow around to starboard. "Looks like the only one left."

He slowed the boat even more so that I could hear the pistons making their slow drumbeat.

A wooden lobster boat and a ketch about forty feet long were the closest boats to us. No one was topside on either boat. Good thing: If I was going to make an idiot of myself again, at least no one would see.

"Get ready," said Dad. "I'll come up to it on the starboard side."

"Okay," I said.

The boat eased her way through the water, the

wavelets smacking against her hull. The mooring ball was only about fifteen feet ahead. Gripping onto the forestay, I crouched and stretched to reach the boathook out as far as I could.

Closer now, Dad slowed the boat even more, and then the engine coughed. It coughed again. I leaned out as far as I could and slashed at the pennant, the line dangling from the ball into the water. I missed. I tried again, the boathook splashing past it.

The boat had almost come to a standstill, leaving me just out of reach of the mooring.

"Bring her forward," I yelled to Dad.

As he eased the throttle up and the boat inched ahead, I stretched out as far as I could and thrust the boathook out at the line. This time I hooked the line, and I yelled, "Got it!" as I kneeled down to bring my other hand onto the boathook. Dad throttled back.

Before I could get a grip, a gust of wind came up. I'd brought the boat broadside to the wind by pulling on the pennant, and now the gust filled the sail and drove us forward hard. I fell down on the deck as the boat surged forward and heeled over.

I gripped onto the boathook, and the boathook still had the mooring line. The boat pressed forward and I slid down the deck.

"Hang on," called Dad.

I was all that kept us attached to the mooring line. The boat had other things in mind.

Dad jumped to the cabintop and banged his knee against the handrail.

"Damn!" he said as he fumbled to release the main halyard.

The boat pulled harder and began to swing around.

I groaned as the line forced me further down the deck. I was losing my grip.

"Dad!" I gasped as the sail slithered and cascaded and piled down, the rigging scraping and whining and the sail hoops clacking and the gaff cracking to the deck beside my ear. I was lost in an avalanche of Dacron.

With the sail down, the boat eased off, and with one hand I flung the sail off me. I saw a lump of sail thrashing. It was Dad, a sailcloth ghost. He thrashed again and heaved the sail off him and scrambled forward to take the boathook from me.

"Got it," he said, panting. He hauled up the dripping line and attached the loop to the bow cleat.

He stood up and ran his hand through his hair. He looked at me and chuckled.

"You did it, Luke," he said. "That was a heroic effort." He clapped me on the back and said, "Let's get squared away and then catch our breath. This has been a heck of a trip."

I was still steamed about what had happened in the channel, and almost losing the boathook wasn't my idea of a smooth maneuver. Now he was calling me a hero, an exaggeration if I ever heard one. I could picture Mom shaking her head, an ironic smile on her face. Beth would have said to me in a mocking voice, "Luke, did I ever tell you you're my hero?"

I was no hero. Dad was no hero, either. But we were stuck with each other just the same.

CHAPTER FOUR:
NANTUCKET ON THE LINE

We furled and covered the sail. I went below and pulled the awning out of the forepeak. We rigged it over the cockpit, draping it over the boom, hoisting it up, and lashing it to the rail so it formed a kind of open tent. Then we cooked dinner and ate topside. It was the usual simple fare that we had when we cruised, this time canned ham doused in rum and fried in a skillet.

As we ate, the sun dropped behind the steeples and rooftops of town and lit the sky a brilliant red, tingeing the neck of sand and scrub beyond us called Coatue with a rosy glow. It was a tentacle of a barrier beach between the Sound and the Head of the Harbor, the body of water that lay to our east. This far out in the mooring field, the waves had a chance to build when the breeze shifted into the southeast and began to puff. *Piper* took on a lively motion.

While we were washing the dishes, Dad asked me if I wanted to go ashore to "see what's doing" and I said sure. Going ashore with Dad wasn't my idea of a great time. But maybe I could go off by myself for a while to snoop around.

He radioed the launch to come pick us up, and we sat in the cockpit to wait. The perfume of beach roses came to me from the land, mingled with the tang of the harbor water and the incense of charcoal smoke. A few boats moved through the harbor and their running lights and the lights of the town danced on the water.

"This is one of my favorite times of the day," said Dad. He was stretched out on a seat cushion, his fingers laced behind his head. I sat the same way on the opposite side of the cockpit. I'd put on a pair of khakis and my yellow chamois shirt because of the evening chill. Harbor sounds came to me, among them the sound of tinkling halyards against aluminum masts and the splash of water against the hull. Now and then a small plane buzzed overhead. The afterglow of the sun still cast a dimming reddish light over us.

"Might as well take advantage of it while we're waiting," he said. He fetched his sketchbook and settled back onto the cockpit seat with his back to the bulkhead.

"We'll have to see what the weather's like tomorrow," he said. "Hey, maybe we'll even sail out to Monomoy, the way you suggested."

"I thought it was too shallow," I said, "and the tides were too strong."

"We can figure it out if we decide to go," he said. "Besides, the shoal water's on the Sound side. The back-side has plenty of water."

Now he's changing his tune, I thought. If it was up to Chet or Mom or Beth or me, we'd be out there right now.

I could hear his pencil sniffing across the page. I wished I could listen to "Thief" instead of Dad drawing.

"Things'll get better, Luke," he said. "Today's trip was more of a shakedown cruise, a sea trial. Things'll go wrong anyway. You have to expect it. Even after you've gotten your sea legs. *Piper*'s not used to us, that's all. We haven't been sailing her enough this year. Soon we'll find the right rhythm, and we'll be handling her like we were born to it. There's an art to sailing, just like there's an art to living. If you don't work at it, you end up floun-dering around."

I rolled my eyes and almost groaned out loud. This kind of thing made me gag. Now I really wished I could blot him out. I felt like I was back at school: The Art of Sailing 101.

The Art of Floundering was more like it.

"I've been meaning to ask you something, Luke," he said.

It was getting worse. I was going to have to put up with the thing I dreaded most: the man-to-man talk. Why couldn't he just draw?

"Have you given much thought to what you want to do?" he said. "Pretty soon you're going to have to make up your mind what kind of college you want to go to, art school or something else. And what about after? Have you given that any thought?"

My shoulders had gone tight and bunched. I noticed that I'd crossed my arms and my legs. Where the hell was that launch?

"No, not really," I said. I tried not to sound morose, but the "no" came out sounding like a cow mooing.

"Well, I wouldn't recommend you being an art director like me," he said. "Especially a freelancer. Too many bosses to take orders from."

He lifted his pencil from the paper. "But you," he said, "you should take after your mom. You've got the gift."

I wasn't in the mood for a lecture about my future— not that I ever was. And I sure didn't want to hear how I should take after Mom, not right now. She was the reason I was stuck on the boat with Dad. She was the reason I had to listen to his "advice."

Besides, I didn't think I had any kind of gift. Sure, I loved to sketch and paint, and many times over the years I had gone into Mom's studio to see what she was doing and listen to her tell me about how she was going about a painting, but a gift? No, Beth had the gift. Her paintings were different from Mom's, more delicate, but you could see they had a touch to them—clean, precise, orderly, luminous. No wonder she was in Florence. But sometimes I wondered if even she knew she had the gift. Just before she left for Italy, she said to me, "I've always envied your style of drawing. It's loose, carefree. I look at what I do and then look at yours, and mine looks constipated. Too studied. I hope Italy will change things."

"It's just something for you to think about, Luke," he went on. "Stay in the habit of drawing. You'll be a junior this year and college is coming up fast."

I heard the burble of an engine and saw running lights approaching.

Sweet, I thought. Saved by the launch.

I stood up to catch the line, and then I saw who was at the helm: the girl I'd seen on the Friendship sloop, out in the channel, wearing the same Red Sox hat and now a bright orange fleece to keep off the chill. She probably thought I was a moron. I tried to think of an excuse not to go, to duck below as fast as I could.

She said a bright "Hi!" as she spun the launch around and held it evenly next to our deck.

"How are you guys doing tonight?" she said as we climbed aboard. Dad and I sat down, and Dad draped his arm along the rail.

"Never better," he said.

She looked over her shoulder as she backed us off

Piper. Then she put it into forward and swung us around toward the wharf. "Great sailing today, wasn't it?"

"We just got here from the Cape this afternoon," said Dad. "It was a fantastic sail."

"Yeah, I saw you coming in." She throttled up and we cruised our way through the moored boats. "You were out by the jetties when we passed you. I was crewing on *Endeavor*."

Dad said, "She's one lovely vessel."

Here it comes, I thought. She would probably ask me why I'd almost wrecked the boat. Have some trouble out there? she'd probably ask.

But all she said was, "Sure is. Sometimes I fill in for my brother if he wants a day off to fish or something. Where're you two headed?"

Dad smiled at her. "Luke here and I are sailing wherever the wind takes us. And you? Will you be out again tomorrow?"

How gross, I thought. I know what he's doing. He's actually flirting with her—a girl about my age.

I elbowed him in the ribs.

"Hey!" he said.

"Sorry," I said. "That wave made me do it."

"Doesn't look like the sailing's going to be too great tomorrow," she said. "Tonight it's supposed to blow and pour right through tomorrow morning."

"That's too bad," said Dad. I saw him turn toward me. "I may have to throw Luke overboard to keep him from going stir crazy."

We passed the last of the moorings and crossed the main channel before the wharves. She waved at a big black-hulled dragger heading in, and the helmsman waved back through the pilothouse window. When she throttled down near the dock, she said, "Luke" in such a definite voice I almost jumped off the seat. "Luke, if you're here for a while and you get cabin fever, a bunch of us are always hanging out at the ice cream place just above the launch dock. You should come by."

I managed to say "Thanks," and took a quick look at her. She was smiling, her eyes on the water ahead.

"My name's Cass," she said. "Cass Garrett."

She backed us to the wharf, stepped off with the line, and looped it around the piling.

"Remember," she said. "Last launch leaves at three."

"If we're not back here by ten," said Dad as he handed her a twenty, "send out a press gang."

Cass laughed. "You can count on it," she said, looking at the bill. "The fee's only five dollars."

Dad waved his hand. "Keep it," he said.

"Friendly girl," said Dad as we walked along the cobblestones on Straight Wharf. "She had her eye on you, Luke."

"I don't think so," I said.

"Sure she did," he said, bumping me with his shoulder. "Maybe you should ask her to join us."

"Cut it out, Dad," I said, grimacing. "I didn't have my eye on her. You did."

He chuckled.

"No, not really," he said.

"Admit it, Dad. You did."

"I'll admit she's pretty cute. But you think she even knew I was there? No way, buddy. I'm telling you, she thinks you're hot. But Ginnie might not be too happy about it."

My impulse was to clam up, and I wished I'd listened to it. But for some reason I said, "Ginnie and I aren't going out," and the moment I did, I wished I hadn't.

I could tell he had raised his eyebrows even though I wasn't looking at him when he said, "Ah, I see. Now we really are two castaway pirates, adrift like flotsam and jetsam."

"Not really," I said.

"Oh, sure," he said with that self-amused tone. "You're Flotsam and I'm Jetsam. Or is it the other way around? But now you're free to go have an ice cream with Cass."

Saying anything else would only encourage him, so I kept quiet even though I was seething. He let it drop.

We walked along, stepping out of the way of the

milling tourists who were eating ice cream cones and goggling at the brightly lit shop windows. Underfoot the ground felt like it was rolling after our day on the water. The smells of frying food and beer and perfume and rank fishy harbor water coming to us on the moist breeze almost overwhelmed me. The trees, dark now in the dusk, rustled and hissed in the growing wind.

We poked into a couple of stores selling T-shirts, another selling nautical junk, and a couple of art galleries that Dad lingered in. All I knew was that I wanted to keep moving. I didn't see any paintings that rivaled Mom's or Beth's stuff, or even Dad's, for that matter, but in one shop Dad was taken with the sailor's valentines and bird carvings. "They're art forms that demand delicacy and strength," he said, "both in the artist and the art."

"Dad," I said, trying to head off another lecture, "I think the place is closing."

He emerged from his reverie and glanced at me.

"Let's get going, then," he said. "I can see you're in a rush to catch a bus."

Wandering down Union Street, we passed a bank of public phones. Dad stopped in front of them.

"Do you want to call your mother?" he said. "Might be kind of novel for you to call her from a pay phone on Nantucket. I actually called her from one of these very phones before we were married. All you have to do is call information and get the number for Lucy Talbot, the Wicked Witch of Downeast, Little Spruce Island, Maine. When your mother picks up, you can say, 'Mrs. Jane Emerson? Just a moment, Nantucket on the line.'"

"What, are you serious?" I said.

"She might like to talk to you. Give her a break from listening to the Wicked Witch go on about her quilts."

"No, I don't think so."

It felt as though she had vanished, gone to a place where she was as unreachable as if she'd traveled to the deepest undersea trench. I didn't think there was any way to reach her—not even on her cell phone. And besides, what did I have to say to her? Sure, I missed her, but she left me, too, didn't she?

"Why do you call Aunt Lucy that, anyway?"

"The Wicked Witch?" He paused, then chuckled. "Because she can't stand me. Never could. She started it, not to sound petty. When your mom and I were first married, I answered the phone one time. Lucy asked for Jane, and she didn't know that I hadn't hung up yet. When your mom got on the other line, she said, 'So how's life with the Cartoonist?' The Talbot sisters were always quite a team."

Everything seemed beyond me. Mom's leaving was

confusing enough. Now it was beginning to seem stupid and selfish.

To think of her there with Aunt Lucy, probably not giving us a passing thought, somehow made me furious. It was as though it was already nearly normal—for everyone but me.

"You sure you don't want to call?" Dad said.

"I'm sure," I said. "Stop asking me."

I strode off down the cobblestones, not turning around to see if he was following. I speed-walked up one side of Main Street and down the other, staring lightning bolts at the asinine oblivious sunburned tourists herding around, until my anger finally began to cool. I slowed down and found a bench and sat down. After a few minutes, I saw Dad walking up the sidewalk, his hair yellowish under the dim streetlights. He was pretending to window shop, clasping his hands behind his back as he peered in the windows. He pulled on his ratty striped sailing sweater and ambled toward me along the lumpy brick sidewalk. His aimlessness and slouchy nautical air made him look out of place among the tourists.

He's a lost soul, I thought. My father is a wreck without Mom.

"I don't know about you, but I'm kind of hungry," he said when he walked up to me. "Guess the salt air got my appetite going. Want to get a bite before we head back to the boat?"

"Yeah," I said. "That sounds good."

We pushed our way into a place on the wharf called The Ropewalk. Dad had a martini and I had a lemonade while we waited for a plate of littlenecks on the half shell. The bar was crowded, and all the noise and heat and ruckus got on my nerves. I was dog-tired. The bruises I'd gotten falling all over the boat began to ache and throb. I touched my hand to the rope burn on my face.

"You look the way I feel," said Dad as he set his glass down. The waitress brought the littlenecks, and Dad ordered another drink.

"Pretty lively in here," he said to her. "You'd never know it was the end of the season."

"Tell me about it," she said, hustling off.

We finished the clams and Dad drained his drink.

"Let's have another one," he said, "and then shove off."

I shrugged. "Sure," I said.

He ordered another, and another after that. We sat in silence as he drank, the crowd noise overwhelming us. The voices throbbed and swelled. I looked around the room and I glimpsed a girl with red hair that was the same color as Ginnie's. For a moment I thought, What's she doing here? Then she turned and I saw that she looked nothing like Ginnie, but longing speared me just the same. The reasons I'd refused to draw her became misty. What had I been thinking? Why hadn't I drawn her?

"Want another?" he said.

I was about to burst with lemonade.

"Nope," I said. "I'm all set."

"You sure? I could use another one."

I looked at him. His eyes were glassy and bright—four martinis' worth.

"No, I just told you. I'm all set. Let's go."

"Say no more," he said, holding up his hand. "Sorry if I offended your finer sensibilities."

He flagged the waitress and paid the bill. As we walked along the wharf to the launch, I noticed that he seemed to be considering each step as if he wanted to avoid stepping on scorpions.

A large silent kid about my age was at the helm of the launch. I didn't ask about Cass. The wind had come up all evening and now there was a rising chop as we shoved off. Dad rocked with the motion, his hands held between his knees. He stared into the gloom and his hair fluttered in the wind. Soon we idled up to our boat, and the launch bumped up against *Piper*'s hull. Dad handed me his wallet and nodded toward the kid. I got out a five, paid him, and gave the wallet back. Then I jumped aboard and stepped into the cockpit.

I turned around to hold my hand out to Dad and he was already leaping across the gap between the boats. I didn't know whether to open my arms to him or dodge out of his way. I was frozen as he hurtled toward me.

The toe of his moccasin caught the rubrail and he dropped as if he'd been hit from behind with a sledge-hammer. His momentum carried him forward beneath the awning and he knocked me against the opposite cockpit seat. He ended up cantilevered beneath the tiller as if he'd plunged headfirst into a well.

"You all right over there?" called the kid from the launch.

Why the hell was Dad trying so hard to embarrass me? About the only good thing was that I wasn't hurt. I didn't know about Dad. I waved and yelled, "No problem. Thanks." The launch throttled up and headed away.

I looked down at Dad.

"Wash that last step," he mumbled. A strange low wheezing sound came from him as he started to untangle himself. I got ahold of his arm and tried lifting him up, but because he was belly down, none of his parts would bend the right way.

"You've got to spin around," I said.

The wheezing sound got louder. At first I was alarmed, but then I realized that it was a continuous series of wheezing chuckles, chuckles that soon broke into a salvo of uncontrolled guffaws that sounded like a dog barking.

There was my dad, his legs sticking into the air over the rail, laughing so hard rigor mortis had set in. His laughter infected me, too. Thinking of the sight of him diving into the cockpit and his slurring of "Watch that last step" sparked my own laughter.

At last he got himself somewhat under control and he climbed out of the cockpit as if wading through deep sludge. He slipped on the companionway stairs and then threw himself on his bunk, where a fit of laughter overtook him again.

I lit the oil lamp. It was a mellower light than the stark overhead cabin light, and the cabin took on a warm golden glow. Dad quieted down, but by the time I took off my clothes, blew out the light, and melted into my sleeping bag on the opposite berth, I heard a new sound coming from him.

The sound made me clench my teeth together in disgust. It was the sound of sobbing. My eyes snapped open when I realized what I was hearing. My heart began to thunder—to thunder with revulsion at him for becoming a blubbering mass, to thunder with anger at him for dragging me away, anger at my mother for flicking us away like a pair of worthless ants.

"Dad!" I said, but the sobbing went on.

I couldn't stand it.

I got out of my sleeping bag, switched on the overhead cabin light, and got back into my clothes. I reached into my seabag for my sweater and I felt the bag of firecrackers.

I grabbed the bag and a box of matches from the galley drawer, and went topside.

I fished my hand into the paper bag and drew out one of the firecrackers Chet and I had concocted: a 10-gauge shotgun shell, the brass removed, that we had packed with gunpowder. He and his dad reloaded their own shotgun shells for duck and goose hunting, so he had ready access to shells and gunpowder. He used the goosegun shells because they packed more of a wallop than 12-gauge shells. He'd used a soldering iron to close the plastic ends, leaving a short fuse curling out of a hole that he'd cored in the middle.

Putting an end to Dad's sobbing was all I wanted, and when I struck a match my first thought was to light the fuse and toss the bomb like a hand grenade into the cabin.

The thought transfixed me as I touched the match to the fuse. I imagined him flinging himself out of his berth, his face scorched black, his singed hair spiked out and smoking, his clothes hanging in tatters from his powder-burned body.

"Why, Luke?" he called to me in my imagination. "Why did you do it?"

The fuse sizzled down almost instantly and the flame scorched my fingertips. I jerked the firecracker overboard and in one second a cannon shot blasted off and a yellow flash seared the darkness and the raw burnt stench of blown gunpowder swept past me in a cloud of acrid smoke. It was so close I'd felt its heat and the pulse of its concussion.

My ears rang and I coughed and gagged. The firecracker had gone off only a few feet from the hull.

Stupid, I thought. What did I do to the boat? Someone would report this to the harbormaster for sure.

I went below, my ears clanging. The explosion hadn't roused Dad. But at least he had turned over and was muttering to himself, not sobbing.

I got the flashlight and went back topside and trained the beam on the side of the boat. A black powder burn fanned out on the white paint.

Stupid, stupid, stupid. I took the bag of firecrackers out of my pocket and heaved it off the stern. I heard it splash into the water.

It took me the better part of an hour to scrub off the blast stain with a cleaner and an abrasive sponge. Gradually the ringing in my ears subsided and my hearing returned. I had to hold the flashlight in my left hand to see what I was doing with my right. I kept expecting a searchlight to rivet me, and a voice through a megaphone to say, "Don't move, you there on *Piper*." But the harbormaster didn't materialize, and by the time I cleaned up and went below again, my hands quivering, and my brain swimming with fatigue, Dad had pulled his sleeping bag over him. He was sleeping quietly.

I could picture Beth saying in her deadpan way, "So much for a career in the bomb squad."

The rhinoceros thundered after me, roaring through its smile, galumphing into and knocking over an acacia tree, kicking up clouds of dust, roaring and roaring and roaring closer to me until I woke up in the dark of the cabin to the sound of my father snoring louder than anything I'd ever heard in my life. The gap between our berths was no more than three feet.

"Dad! Dad! Wake up!" I stage-whispered. I heard him turn over, but he kept on snoring. I got up and switched on the cabin light. He lay under his sleeping bag with his face crushed down on his pillow, his mouth mashed open. I yelled at him again, but even though he jumped and mumbled and turned to the other side, he kept right on snoring, if anything with even more gusto than before. He snored with a kind of vengeance. Not even Mel's snoring rivaled Dad's.

I switched off the light and crawled into my sleeping bag. Nothing I tried would let me go back to sleep, so finally I got dressed again and tossed my sleeping bag into the cockpit. I crawled topside to spread it on one of the seats and wriggled inside. I could still hear him, but the gagging and snorting weren't quite as thunderous. The wind had come on strong and a drizzle fell, swirling with the gusts. The awning helped keep most of it off me. I didn't mind feeling the cool of the drizzle on my face now and then as *Piper* swung on her mooring into the wind. Beyond the stern, I watched the lights of the moored boats, the wharves and town beyond, and the sweep of Brant Point Light.

I figured I'd never get back to sleep, thoughts of Mom and Monomoy and Ginnie and Dad swarming through my mind and my heart speeding in my chest. But soon my eyes were drooping as I was lulled by the sound of the water lapping against the hull and the easy movement of *Piper* jogging at her mooring.

CHAPTER FIVE:
A CALL TO THE SEA

I winced when my eyes snapped open to see a beam of light rake over me. How long I'd been asleep, I couldn't tell. I felt *Piper* yawing and rocking through heavier waves than before. My instinct was to pull the sleeping bag over my head to make the light go away. But I heard a boat motor idling. My heart accelerated.

"Hello there, *Piper*!" called a voice from the direction of the beam of light. "Anyone aboard *Piper*?"

Jesus, it's the harbormaster flashed through my mind as I kicked my way out of the sleeping bag. But when I held my hand against the light, I made out the shape of a sailboat.

That wouldn't be the harbormaster. He'd be in a powerboat.

I stuck my head below.

"Dad!" I yelled. "Someone's out there!" I was still in a near coma and I didn't know what was going on. I felt below for the light switch and flipped it on.

"*Piper*!" came the voice again. "Can I tie up to you for the night?"

"Whus going on?" said Dad, rolling to a sitting position and rubbing his face.

"Someone's out there, a boat, says he wants to tie off our stern," I said.

"Okay," he said, swinging his legs to the deck. He fought aside the sleeping bag, staggered as he stepped into his shorts, sat back down on the berth, then lurched to his feet. His hair stuck out at crazy angles as if he'd been electrocuted. Sleep-creases crinkled his cheek.

The boat idled beside us. From the beams of the lighthouse, I could make out small whitecaps passing and the boat riding over the steepening chop. It was a sloop somewhat bigger than us.

Dad bumped into the cockpit. "Throw me a line," he called to the boat. By the intermittent light, I could see that the man on the boat was wearing full orange oilskins. He brought the boat beside us, grabbed a coil of line, and bounded to the deck to toss it to Dad. Then he staggered forward, made the other end of the line fast to the forward cleat, and let his boat drift back behind us.

Dad tied the line to both cleats on the stern and then waved to the man.

The man stood at the bow. "No other moorings free," he called. "Too tight in here to anchor in this blow. Thanks for your help." He waved and made his way to the cockpit, then disappeared below.

Dad stood for a moment, scratching his head and yawning. The wind whined in the rigging, and the waves made a continuous splashing sound as they washed over each other.

"Guess he'll be fine back there," said Dad. "Plenty of room between the other boats." The man reappeared and went forward to tie an anchor light to his forestay.

"Time to go back to sleep," said Dad. "Why were you topside, anyway?"

I blinked at the boat riding off our stern. The cold was getting to me, and I decided I'd try sleeping in my berth below again. Telling him about the firecracker wouldn't make much sense.

"I had to come up here," I said, "because there was a rhinoceros down below."

"Sorry about that, Luke," he said as he eased himself down the companionway steps. "Hit me with a pillow if I do it again."

"How about an anchor," I said.

"Whatever works."

I followed him below with my sleeping bag, spread it on the berth, crawled into it, and fell asleep before my mind started churning.

Days later, it seemed, I woke to the sound of rain clattering like pebbles against the portholes. I'd been so tired that the minute I'd closed my eyes, I'd blacked out. Not even the rhino had roused me.

I rolled over and blinked. Gray daylight filled the cabin, admitted by the rain-marbled portholes. I smelled fresh coffee. I looked over and saw the pot on the stove. Dad's sleeping bag lay rumpled on his berth. From topside, I heard voices. I sat up and looked through the companionway hatch.

Dad was sitting under the awning, wearing his yellow oilskins, holding a mug of coffee. Another guy, an old guy, sat on the opposite side of the cockpit.

"There he is," said Dad, looking at me. "Thought you'd never wake up. Come on up, Luke, and meet our next-door neighbor."

I put on my jeans and fleece and oilskins and climbed into the cockpit.

I glanced at Dad. His face looked pale, almost gray, and his stubble seemed to have gotten an extra growth of scruffiness. I wondered if he even remembered what had gone on during the night.

"This is Gus," said Dad. "Gus Sinclair. Gus, this is Luke, my first and only mate."

I shot him a look.

"Good to meet you, Luke," said Gus, grinning at me. He stooped under the awning and leaned forward to shake my hand. He was small and wiry and had a

tight grip. His eyebrows were two black inverted paren-
theses, and below them were two sky-blue eyes. With
his hood up, he looked like an elf peering out of a cave.

The rain slanted down, clattering against the awning,
and the wind whipped up whitecaps and bowed the
awning like a sail when it gusted.

"Gus brought us over some coffee," said Dad.

"As a thank you," said Gus, "for saving me the trouble
of having to find good holding ground last night."

"Get yourself a mug," said Dad, looking at me. "It's
fresh from Cuba." Our eyes met, and I held his gaze.
In that moment I knew he knew what had happened
during the night. Thank God Gus was there or Dad
would have said something the way he had the morning after the frame-throwing. It was hard to believe
that had only been the day before yesterday. Now we
had had another blowup, a real one, and he could have
given me grief about it. But he would have to let it pass.

"Best coffee I've tasted in ages," he said. "You know
what they say about forbidden fruits."

Gus chuckled. "Not forbidden to Canadians."

"True. So you were saying you were headed for the
Caribbean," said Dad as I went below to fill a mug.

"My plan was to sail down there," said Gus, "but I
had . . . I had a change of heart. I'm on my way home
now."

I climbed back up and sat in the companionway and sipped my coffee. I watched Gus's boat ride and bob on her line behind us, running first one way, then the other with the gusts. The Canadian ensign snapped from her backstay. She was a wooden sloop, rough around the edges with peeling paint on her hull and her spars in need of varnish. She had a tanbark mainsail, a traditional scab-red color you didn't see very often, and it was loosely furled so that parts of it flapped in the gusts. But she looked solid and the sweep of her bow made her look eager to get going. I wondered why Gus changed his plans.

"Is that a Folkboat you have there?" asked Dad.

"That's right," said Gus, sipping his coffee. "She's a Cheoy Lee, built in Hong Kong in 1959. My wife and I bought her from her original owner ten years ago. We always planned to sail down to the Caribbean once we retired."

He looked into his mug as if he saw something deep inside it.

"She does have beautiful lines," said Dad.

Gus gazed back at the boat. "She does indeed. But I've found on the trip here from Nova Scotia that my heart isn't in it anymore. The Caribbean, that is."

He sighed and looked at us. "I've discovered that it's back home, in Rose Bay."

He shook his head and laughed. "Cruising the Caribbean was something that Louise and I had always said we'd do. I thought that after she passed away I'd make the trip for the two of us."

He sipped his coffee.

"I stopped in anchorages all along the Maine coast," he said, "and beautiful cruising ground it is. But the more distance I put between us, the lonelier I grew."

He chuckled. "I made it down to Marblehead and through the Cape Cod Canal. But once I got to Cuttyhunk, I had to face it. I just didn't want to keep going without Louise. But instead of just abandoning the trip I thought I'd stop in Edgartown, and then make the crossing to Nova Scotia. I was on my way home when the weather got other ideas. I had to run for cover, and luckily I wasn't far from Nantucket. But not a mooring to be had, either. That's when I found you. I couldn't help but want to tie up to you when I saw that the name of your boat was *Piper*."

He paused. The wind rattled the awning and *Piper* swung on her mooring.

"Not a year ago," he said, "my nephew played the pipes at Louise's funeral—she was a Robertson—and I took it as a kind of sign seeing your boat's name in my spotlight."

No one said anything. The wind hummed in the rigging and raindrops dripped from the edge of the awning.

"I've always wanted to sail," said Dad, "to sail without anything weighing me down. But I guess that's not possible."

Gus looked at him for a moment. Then he chuckled.

"There's always something you left behind to worry about, eventually, even though at times sailing takes so much concentration there's no room to think about anything else."

Dad nodded. "I know what you mean."

Gus sipped his coffee. "Where are you two headed?"

"After here, the Vineyard, maybe the Elizabeths," said Dad. "If we have time. Do the reverse of your trip."

"And we might sail to Monomoy," I said, "just to do some exploring."

"A wonderful cruise for a father and son," said Gus. "You've sailed these waters a lot?"

"Since I was a kid," said Dad.

I started to say that I had been, too, but I stopped myself. It might sound stupid.

"When I left," Gus said, "I thought I'd head to Bermuda first, and I was going to set a course through the Gulf Stream, something I've always wanted to see again. But I thought better of it, and stuck to gunkholing."

He paused when the rain clattered against the awning and *Piper* swung on her mooring. I pictured him going down the coast from cove to cove, always ghosting in alone, always thinking of the Gulf Stream, of Rose Bay, always longing for his lost wife.

"Long ago, I crewed on a yawl in the Bermuda Race," he said, his voice growing soft. "We sailed through the Gulf Stream. The Gulf Stream . . . it still fascinates me to this day."

He looked at me. "It amazed me then, when I was probably not much older than you, Luke. It's got a different color, smell, feel. It's an immense river of water, flowing its own way in the ocean. Sometimes currents split off and revolve in great circles, trapping whatever's inside them forever."

He laughed and looked back at his boat.

"The time I crewed, I saw two sailboats within sight of each other carried in opposite directions, drifting away from each other even though they were on the same tack."

I watched him as he fell silent. He looked out at the water beyond his boat, his mug held loosely in his hands.

Something about his description of the Gulf Stream lit a curl of flame in my chest, a sharp pang of heat that made me want to go, not only to Monomoy but far beyond. Beyond to the Gulf Stream. Maybe that was where I'd find the Big Freedom.

Dad didn't say anything. I glanced at him. He was

leaning back, watching Gus, his forehead furrowed with three wavy lines. No one said anything for a moment. The halyard rapped against the mast and the waves clucked against the hull and the boat jogged and bobbed.

I wondered, Was he thinking the same thing I was? About going out there? Somehow concentrating on heading out had pushed all my other problems aside. I hadn't thought of Mom or Ginnie or even Dad himself since Gus started telling his story.

Gus peered under the awning.

"Soon as this lets up," he said, "I'm off for home, straight across the Gulf of Maine. If you don't mind me using you as my anchor till then, that is."

"No problem at all," said Dad.

"Thank you, then," he said.

"And thank you for the coffee," said Dad.

Gus stood up and shook Dad's hand, then mine. He climbed onto the deck, stepped on the line to haul his boat up to us, and jumped aboard. As the boat drifted back, he raised his arm and called to us, "Sorry for bending your ear so much." Then he climbed around to the companionway hatch and disappeared below.

I woke with a distant moaning in my ears. The cabin was dark. I had no idea what time it was, but I could tell that the wind had shifted and the rain had stopped at last after an entire day of dismal light, driving rain, and drumming winds. After Gus's visit the day before we'd idled, holing up in *Piper*'s confines. Dad had dozed and sketched and cooked for us. I'd done some sketching myself. The sea trials and the night ashore had worn us out. When I checked to see how Gus's boat was riding off our stern, I could see a warm yellow glow coming from the portholes. But Gus stayed below.

I could have gone over to the wharf to see if Cass was around, but I kept putting it off. I was tired, I told myself. But the truth was that I was feeling shy, too. My excuse was that I was too worn-out and banged up, and besides, I couldn't get Ginnie out of my mind.

I heard only the rapid lapping of the water against the hull as *Piper* shifted on her mooring even as I strained my ears for what I thought had been moaning. Through a porthole I saw a star wobble through a break in white clouds. I caught a breath of fresh dry air.

I heard the moaning again. Was that the long mournful cry of a great black-backed gull? Or was that the sound of bagpipes I was hearing?

I thought that it must be Gus. Maybe he was a piper himself, and he was standing on deck, playing the pipes, thinking of his wife back in Nova Scotia.

But then I heard the canvas awning flutter and crack,

and I realized that I had been hearing the wind moaning through our stays. The wind had shifted, probably a big northwest wind to chase away the gloom.

I was nestling under my sleeping bag when the wind moaning in the rigging was joined by another sound, one that made me shake my head in disgust.

I heard the first snort, cough, and sputter coming from the berth beside me. While the wind was scouring the air clean, the rhinoceros had returned. At first I thought I couldn't even close my eyes, but the wind lifted my thoughts out to the Gulf Stream, where the rolling swell carried me off to sleep.

CHAPTER SIX:
BEYOND MONOMOY

Reflected sunlight rippled across the cabin ceiling when I woke up in the morning. Blue sky showed in the portholes and the companionway, and fresh dry air breathed over me.

"Look at this day!" said Dad when I climbed into the cockpit. He was already untying the awning. "Breeze lay down overnight so we won't even have to reef the sail. What do you say we get an early start?"

I said sure. I was still groggy, but the cool air flowing over the shimmering water tried its best to sweep my head free of cobwebs. The chill raised gooseflesh on my arms. Then I noticed.

"Where's Gus?" I said.

"Here, take this," said Dad, handing me one of the lines we used to lash down the awning. "He took off at first light. Told me to tell you good luck. He's at the wharf now, over at the town dock, fueling up."

We folded the awning, and Dad said he'd stow it below.

"I meant to ask you," he said, stopping at the top step. "Did you catch the name of his boat?"

"No," I said. "I never did."

"*Lucky Stars*," he said. "Seems a bit ironic. Luck wasn't on his side when it came to his wife, was it?"

"I guess not."

He went below with the awning while I stayed topside. Sunlight shattered off the water and pillowcase clouds sailed across the laundered sky. Flags and burgees snapped in the breeze and gulls teetered and veered high above the mastheads. A few sailboats were already out, heeling their way through the water.

I wished I'd seen Gus before he cast off. I wanted to ask him more about the Gulf Stream, to hear about what he'd seen out there.

But it was time for us to go. Dad came back topside and I went back below to get ready.

"Where are we headed?" I said, putting on my shorts.

Dad looked up at the sky and then turned to look at me. "Just about anywhere would be fine on a day like this, wouldn't it?" he said. "I know we said we were going to the Vineyard, but now I'm not so sure. Maybe we will head to Monomoy after all. We can always anchor up for the night off the island and head over to the Vineyard tomorrow."

I felt like saying, You're full of it. There's no way we're going. Don't tantalize me.

"Whatever," I said as I put on my shirt. "Anywhere's fine."

I pulled my sweatshirt on and looked topside to catch him watching me. He seemed about to say something, but changed his mind.

"Let's get some breakfast, then," he said. "We'll head out after that."

"Okay," I said. Right, I thought. Good-bye, Monomoy.

Dad started the engine and it cranked up with a gruff rattle and idled with a purr.

"Sounds good," he said. "You can let us go whenever you're ready."

I went forward and uncleated the mooring line, looked back at Dad, got the nod, and tossed the line overboard. Dad put the boat into gear and bore off, heading toward the channel.

"We'll motor out beyond the jetties and then get the sail up," he called from the cockpit. "We'll have the wind almost on the nose going out."

We weaved our way through the mooring field, the waves in the harbor slapping at our hull. I looked for Gus's boat at the wharf but I couldn't pick it out among the other boats. *Piper* clipped along solid and stately. It was a good feeling to be heading out, no matter where we were headed.

The launch came around the end of the wharf as we were making our turn into the channel. Dad throttled up and turned the boat toward Brant Point. I squinted at the launch, and I saw Cass at the helm. She had the launch slipping along at a good pace and passed within a few yards of our stern. No passengers were aboard. She must have been on a run to pick up someone from a moored boat.

She raised her arm and waved it back and forth when she saw us.

"Have a good trip!" she called. "See you again some-time!"

I waved back.

When I glanced back at Dad, I saw him lift his hand to his heart, clutch it, close his eyes, and stagger backward against the cockpit seat in a pantomime swoon.

I shook my head and turned back to look at the channel and the Sound beyond.

We were early enough to beat the parade of boats that would be heading out and made it through the channel before eight o'clock. I hoisted the sail and Dad cut the engine.

I noticed by the compass that we were on a north-northeast heading—one that would take us to Monomoy.

"So where're we headed?" I said as I sat down on the cockpit seat.

"Where's it look like we're headed?"

I checked the compass again.

"Well, it looks like we could be headed for Monomoy."

"Monomoy Point to be exact," he said, and looked at me. "What, you don't believe me?"

I had to laugh.

"No, no, I believe you now," I said. And I thought, Sweet. Maybe this won't be so bad after all. At least we're going where I want to go for once.

I looked over at Dad to see him smiling at nothing in particular.

As we bounded across the Sound, the morning opening up bright and warm before us, Dad tuned in the marine weather on the radio. The report was for clear dry weather for the next few days. The forecaster said a low pressure system would develop in a day or two, but that it would track to our south.

Great Point Light stood like a small white post to our southeast and I picked up the first miragelike forms of Monomoy. I took the tiller from Dad, and he stretched out on the cockpit seat, his back against the bulkhead, his hands laced behind his head. With the wind out of the northwest, we were on a beam reach, *Piper*'s best point of sail, with an easy helm and not much heeling. He looked out over the sparkling blue water.

"Didn't I tell you that things would shape up?" he said, squinting at me in the sunshine. "What a gem of a day, and everything running as smooth as can be."

Piper cantered through the easy swells. The island grew before us, and soon I could make out the biscuit-colored beaches and scrub-covered dunes. The gulls and terns flapped above the beach like confetti. I thought of my trip to the island with Mom, and I wished she were here so we could talk about it together.

"Let's go round the Point and head up the backside of the island," said Dad.

We sailed around the Point into the Atlantic, the ocean stretching away blue and smooth on one side and the island, looking desolate with its low bluffs and beaches, running along our other side. This was the place that gave me such a thrill—the zone between a desert island and the great ocean. The island was eerie and remote, and the ocean was beautiful and vast and dangerous.

We sailed for about an hour along the shore, passed the break separating the two islands, then came about and ran back toward the Point.

"It was right around here that you used to be able to see the wreck of the *Pendleton*," said Dad. By then, we were about three-quarters of the way down the length of the southern island. "Its huge rusting stern used to jut out of the water at an angle like this," he said, tilting his hand at forty-five degrees. "The rail was lined with cormorants waiting to dive on fish, and the current created whirlpools around it so that your boat would spin in circles."

"You used to come out here?" I said.

"Yeah," he said. "A long time ago when I spent some time on Nantucket, and I sailed out here with a buddy."

It struck me how odd it was that the two of us could be so similar, both drawn to a remote island by some need for freedom or escape.

"Did you see how Gus's eyes lit up," he said after a while, "when he was talking about sailing in the Bermuda Race?"

"Yeah," I said, "sounded pretty good to me."

He sat up and looked toward the island.

"Me, too," he said, looking the other way, toward the open ocean. For a few moments he didn't move, staring with such intensity that I thought he had spotted something out there.

Then he stretched back out and closed his eyes to the sun. We sailed on, the motion and the quiet creak of the rigging and thump of the sail and the strong sunshine soothing me. Dad's head began to sway with the motion of the boat and I thought he slipped off to sleep. The ocean sparkled in the sun, and the sight of it was a magnet to me. It drew me to it and made me want to see what was beyond the horizon.

Maybe that was what Dad had felt, too.

Off to starboard, the top of the abandoned lighthouse appeared above a dune. I watched it ride along the crest of the dune as we coasted past the island.

Then Dad opened his eyes.

"We could do it, you know," he said.

We topped a small wave and our wake made a sizzling sound of applause behind us.

"Do what?" I said.

"Sail out," he said. "Sail out to the Gulf Stream."

I looked at him.

"Are you serious?" I said. I couldn't believe that he'd want to do something so crazy. Maybe he had been drawn to wild places when he was younger, but now?

"Sure I'm serious. With this breeze, we'll be out there tomorrow. Then we can cut south of Nantucket and head to the Vineyard through Muskeget Channel."

"You're just kidding me, aren't you?" I said. "We're not really going to go."

We were passing Monomoy Point. Getting so close to its deserted shores always gave me an unsettled feeling. The motion of the water had shifted to show the contrary currents that flowed through the shoals. A rip of wavelets ran like low rapids off our port bow.

Dad stood up and looked at the beach. Among the cries and shrieks of the gulls and the chitter of the terns we heard the gasp and hiss of an unseen swell reaching the sand. A gray seal poked its head out of the water to peer at us. The sight of it unnerved me. Massive as its head was, it looked nearly human, like a bald giant with huge, sad, intelligent eyes. It blinked at us, then submerged.

"Let's go for it, Luke," said Dad, turning to me. "Let's sail out there and then head to Edgartown afterwards. The forecast never sounded better. And it'll be the voyage of a lifetime for the three of us—you, me, and *Piper*."

I looked at Dad and saw a gleam in his eyes, those bright gray-green eyes. Maybe Gus had gotten to him as much as he'd gotten to me. Or maybe he was just trying to prove something. Maybe running away from the mess ashore was what was driving him.

Almost breathless with excitement, he whispered, "Let's keep sailing. We have all the time in the world to see what's out there, and who knows when we'll get another chance. Bring her around a bit and head toward that buoy."

"How far is it out there?" I asked as I eased the tiller away from me.

"Not far at all," he said, squinting up at the sail. He took the mainsheet and let it out. "A hundred miles or so. With a good breeze like this, it'll take us today and tonight and maybe part of tomorrow. If the breeze holds."

I looked at the horizon. A hundred miles was definitely to the ends of the earth and beyond.

"But if you don't want to," he said, "we'll come about and head the way we planned."

I really wanted to be home so I could go fishing with Chet. I wanted to talk to Ginnie. I wished that Beth were along so I'd have an ally. I really didn't want to be with Dad for so long. I really missed Mom. I really did want to see what was beyond the horizon. But did I really want to venture into the middle of nowhere? Out where the sharks and hurricanes ruled? Now that Dad wanted to go so much, did I?

"Okay," I said. "Let's go. I want to see what's out there."

"Are you sure?"

"Sure I'm sure," I said, suddenly not sure at all. "We can always turn around, right?"

"Right you are," he said, easing the main sheet a few more clicks. "I'll check the chart and throw together some lunch. Bring her a couple points more to the south, okay?"

He went below and took out a chart. While he studied it, I looked around at the openness before us. We moved along as if in a dream. But the span of horizon made me uneasy. The moment we set a course away from land, we seemed to shrink.

When he came back topside carrying a plate of

canned chicken sandwiches, he was wearing his sailing lid cocked back on his head at a devil-may-care angle.

He grinned at me. "Sorry, pal, but if we're going to be bluewater sailors together, you've got to get used to some of my quirks."

"I guess so," I said. "At least there's no one around to see you in it."

He chuckled. "Except a gull or a mermaid or two."

Monomoy was already slipping behind us, and nothing but the slow swell of the sea lay ahead.

It was weird. The moment we passed Monomoy Point and headed into the open Atlantic, it felt as if we were slipping over the back of some sleeping beast.

The breeze held steady as the High Bank of Monomoy shrank behind us. I had been watching it when a single sail appeared in the west, moving toward the island.

"Look, another ragsailor," said Dad, "bound for who knows where."

I watched the sail move along, a tiny flag on the immense sea. It moved closer to us, and I wondered about Gus and when he was headed back to Maine.

"You think that might be him?" I said, "might be Gus?"

He sat up and squinted at the distant sail.

"Looks like a sloop," he said. "Let me get the binoculars."

When he came back topside, he got up on the cabintop and trained the glasses at the sail.

"Sure looks like a Folkboat," he said. "I'll bet he headed out a few hours after us."

At that moment our radio down in the cabin crackled to life.

"*Piper, Piper*," I heard, and then the words broke up. ". . . sailing vessel *Piper*," came the calm voice of Gus Sinclair. "This . . . ailing ves . . . *Lucky Stars. Piper*, is that . . . my southeast bearing south?"

Dad jumped below and grabbed the radio handset.

"Gus, it's *Piper*," he said. "Good to hear your voice." He reached up and adjusted the volume on the radio. For such a clear day, the reception was filled with static.

". . . on a course . . . north by east . . . tomorrow . . ." said Gus. For some reason, his voice was breaking up, so that it was hard to string together the sense of what he was saying. Dad suggested that they try a different channel, but that didn't work, either.

His sail was growing smaller as they tried to talk. At one point, Gus said, ". . . you headed? . . . always turn around . . ."

Dad and I looked at each other, puzzling over what he said.

"Can you repeat that, Gus? Did you say 'Turn around'?"

"Your heading . . . usually you sail in Nantucket Sound."

Dad and I nodded at each other. He meant Nantucket Sound, not turn around.

"Where are we headed? Is that what you asked?"

". . . es."

"We've changed our plans a bit. We've decided to head out to the Gulf Stream. We'll be out there in no more than a day."

There was a long sizzle of static, and then we heard, ". . . dangers of . . . high seas . . . look me up . . . make your way home . . ."

Dad was frowning. He said, "Can't hear you too well, Gus. Gus?" He glanced at me and said, "Maybe it's our receiver. I think I've lost him." Then he spoke into the handset again. "Have a safe passage, Gus. Godspeed."

I heard our sail flap and looked up at it to check the luff. When I looked back, the sail on the horizon was gone, and the only reply on the radio was the wash of static.

Dad hung up the handset and came back topside. He looked concerned, but when he sat back down beside me, he said, "It was good to hear him, wasn't it? Good to hear someone we know out here with us. Imagine, him single-handing across the Gulf of Maine."

He stood up and looked across the water. Then he laid his hand on the tiller beside mine.

"Why don't you take a break," he said, "It's time I took the helm for a while."

* * * *

Monomoy dropped below the horizon behind us, and we passed the Great Round Shoal buoy and pressed on deeper into the Atlantic. The afternoon wore on. We sailed by another buoy that clanged forlornly in the long oceanic swell, a great black-backed gull perched atop it. As the buoy fell astern, the gull made a series of shrieks like a baby squalling.

Piper's shadow lengthened over the swells. The sun set and the sky cooled from a pink swath to purple as the stars shivered on and the distant red lights of the two radio towers on Nantucket slipped below the horizon. We left the rips and shoals of Monomoy and Nantucket Shoals behind, the treacherous waters that had wrecked so many ships over the centuries—Old Man Shoal, Orion, Rose and Crown, Handkerchief, McBlair's, Fishing Rip, Pochet, Davis, Pollock Rip, Stone Horse, Great Round Shoal, Asia Rip.

Then we passed through the Great South Channel, the shipping lanes and cod-fishing grounds. We saw the lights of several vessels scattered along the horizon like stars in motion.

All night we sailed before the wind, getting closer to the Gulf Stream.

The troves of stars and sounds of the sea lifted me into a meditative state of mind. Dad must have felt the same way. We kept mostly silent as we rode the swells that sparkled with starlight. Our wake glowed and flashed with green fiery bioluminescence.

Sometime around midnight, after we'd left the lights of the vessels in the Great South Channel far behind, Dad said, "Do you remember how *Piper* got her name?"

"No, not really," I said. He was a dark form sitting at the tiller, the stars clustering in the sky behind him.

"I thought I told you. Maybe it was when we got the boat. But maybe not. You were just a little guy then."

"I remember that *Piper* was *Miss Martha*, right? And I remember Alden Eastman."

"Right. But let me tell you why we named her *Piper*." He paused, then went on, his voice softening. "Your mom and I sailed out beyond Great Point once. It seems like a long time ago now. I'd been living on Nantucket. She was down there on the island, painting. I was foot-loose, working here and there, adventuring, selling sketches to the tourists, sailing on my buddy Gordie Mayo's sloop. That's the guy I sailed with to Monomoy, to see the *Pendleton*. I loved the feeling of reaching a new world."

He stopped speaking. He stayed silent for so long I thought he wasn't going to go on.

"She and I met at school in Providence," he said finally, his voice quiet. "We'd both just graduated. I'd gone to Nantucket, and we bumped into each other one morning down on Straight Wharf, and the rest of the summer we dated. I made up my mind to ask her to marry me, and I borrowed Gordie's sloop to take her out sailing, make it romantic. I didn't plan it too well. I guess I was too excited. I brought a bottle of champagne and the ring but I was so distracted I forgot food. We made it out to Great Point light and naturally the wind quit. We spent the entire afternoon and evening bobbing around, trying to whistle up a breeze. She was laughing at me because all I could find to eat was an old package of saltines in my duffel bag to have with the champagne, Piper-Heidsieck, which didn't last terribly long. 'They were saved by champagne,' she said sarcastically. So when we bought this boat, we named her for that time."

"When did you ask her?"

"On the boat, after the breeze finally came up a bit. Funny thing was that she said no. She said she was too hungry to give me an answer. I was in a panic, but when we finally got back to the harbor, around nine that night, she said yes after I'd bought her a couple of bowls of chowder."

We sailed along, the rigging's creaks and the trickle and gurgle of the water the only comments.

"Then why . . ." I said, ". . . why are you, why is Mom

with Aunt Lucy in Maine and you're here? Why did she leave?"

Why did she leave us, I thought.

He didn't answer right away. I began to wish I hadn't asked the question.

When he spoke, his voice had changed. It was clipped.

"Luke," he said. "She has her reasons. Things have changed for us. They're just not the same. We don't see eye-to-eye anymore. We always had our differences, but now they're all we have. And now she's decided to change. To change everything. Maybe I fell out of love with her, and she fell out of love with me. You know your mother. When she makes a decision, there's no changing her mind."

He fell silent for a moment, then took a deep breath.

"Maybe I didn't live up to her expectations," he said, almost whispering. "Maybe she didn't live up to mine."

He brushed his hair from his forehead.

"It's tough on you, I know," he said. "When we get back, I'll have to talk to Beth, too. But we'll figure it out. We'll live through it."

He looked at me.

"Don't you see?" he said, brightness returning to his voice. "We're shipmates, Luke. Whether we like it or not. You, Lucky Luke, and me, Ahab Andy."

He was right. We were stuck with each other. I was stuck with him. He was stuck with me.

And then he raised himself up on one hip and loosed three farts that honked against the seat.

"Jeez, Dad," I said.

I couldn't see his expression in the darkness, but I imagined that he looked pleased with himself.

"Must have been that canned chicken and Cuban coffee," he said. "A lethal combination."

He thought he was being funny, but he disgusted me. I shook my head and looked out over the water, wondering why I had to put up with a father who wanted to act like a son. Maybe that was what had driven Mom off to Aunt Lucy's. Maybe too many years of having a kid for a husband drove her batty.

Then I remembered what Gus had said, about why he picked *Piper* to tie up to.

"But you told Gus that you'd named the boat because of bagpipes," I said.

He looked at me.

"What?"

"Back in Nantucket. Gus thought *Piper* was named for bagpipes."

"No, not really. He made the leap himself. He assumed that's what we named her for. I just told you—we named the boat after the kind of champagne we drank that day, Piper-Heidsieck. That's how *Piper* got her name."

That didn't sit right with me. I didn't want to say it, but it was a kind of lie.

"I sure felt bad for him, didn't you?" said Dad. "Losing his wife and his dream."

When I didn't answer, he looked at me.

"What's bugging you?"

"Nothing," I said.

"Then why the tone on such a sterling night?"

I hated it when he used words like "sterling." They made my skin prickle they sounded so pretentious.

"Because you lied to him," I said. "You should have told him the truth."

I could see Dad cock his head. "What truth?" he said. "I didn't say anything. I didn't want to burst his bubble. He was happy with his luck. Why make him think otherwise?"

"I don't know," I mumbled. "It's just not right."

Dad ran his hand over his hair.

"It's tough to live up to your expectations sometimes, Luke," he sighed. "Just remember that things aren't always as black and white as you want them to be. And some things are better left unsaid."

I decided to say nothing for fear of saying the wrong thing. I got up and made my way along the rail to the bow and stood looking out at the dark sea stretched ahead of us and the stars sprinkled right down to the horizon. I dipped and rose with the motion of the boat, sick and tired of finding it so easy to find my father at fault for everything.

"Be careful up there," called Dad. "No one's going overboard on my watch."

The wind became light and variable sometime in the middle of the night. I had been snoozing in the cockpit, and I woke to the racket of slatting rigging and the sloppy action of a sailboat without wind. Dad started the engine, and we held our course. At first it wasn't running right. Every now and then it would race, nearly cut out, and cough. Then it got over its tantrum, smoothed itself out, and ran at a regular throb.

Just after dawn, I saw that we'd entered a different zone. The water had gone from gray green to indigo. Along the horizon, cumulus clouds rose like castles. The water looked slick and alive, showing its motion with dimples and whorls. Streaks of mustard-colored weed flowed past us, and off to starboard a dorado burst out of the water, its rainbow sheen flashing in the damp air.

"It's like we sailed into the tropics," I said.

"Welcome to the Gulf Stream," said Dad, grinning and looking around. "We made good time."

He brought *Piper* into what breeze there was so the sail would go slack. We drifted with the current. More eddies and whorls appeared in the water beside us as though a giant oar had just taken a stroke or something immense and unseen were passing beneath us. The swell rose and fell like slowly flexing muscles.

"We're probably heading east-northeast at about three, maybe four knots," said Dad. "But you'd never know we were moving unless you saw those swirls."

Even the smell was different. It was a soft humid vegetable smell, distinct from the sharp salty smell of the colder water we'd left behind.

"Now that we're here, what do we do?" I asked Dad.

He grinned at me.

"We drift. We look. We draw. And in a bit, I catnap."

I looked around the boat. In the entire circle of the horizon, we were the lone vessel.

"Mind if I draw you?" said Dad, stepping below. "I'd like to show everyone back home what a true bluewater sailor looks like."

Dad's eagerness to do a sketch of me rankled me. I felt like a pet. I wanted to tell him to keep his pencil to himself. He didn't own me. I wasn't his model. Drawing me was stealing something from me. I wanted to draw. I didn't want to be drawn.

Everything was always his decision. Even when we went to Monomoy, it was his decision. And going to the Gulf Stream—his decision. I had no say in anything.

"Yeah, I mind," I said. "I'm busy keeping an eye out for sea monsters."

He chuckled as he came topside with his sketchbook.

"What was that?" he said.

"I said I don't want you to."

He laughed and sat down.

"Cut the crap, Luke. Just stay at the helm. This won't hurt a bit."

I was seething, but what could I do? I was steering the boat. I couldn't exactly leap overboard.

So I screwed up my face into the worst frown I could manage and tried to hold it.

"That's beautiful, Luke," he said. "Such a handsome young man. Give me a three-quarters profile so I don't have to be scorched by your withering look."

I shrugged and looked off to sea.

While he was sketching me, I tried to ignore him by watching the motion of the water and thinking about home, about Ginnie, about the evening we saw the shooting star.

I glanced at Dad, and I met his eyes as his hand worked its way over the page.

"Keep looking at the horizon," he said.

"Aye-aye, Captain Bligh," I said. I saw him lift an eyebrow.

I looked back out at the water, and it occurred to me why I hadn't wanted to draw Ginnie. It scared me. If I drew her, I'd make her a part of me. If I got too close to her, I'd lose more of my freedom.

"That's it," said Dad. "All done. Want to see it?"

I knew how much he'd want me to see what he'd done.

I glanced at him. "Not especially," I said, just to irk him. "I already know what I look like."

He chuckled.

"Come on. I know you're dying to see it."

"Not really."

"Okay, then," he said. "I'm going to draw you again."

I looked at him and saw a playful glint in his eye. I didn't want to egg him on.

I held out my hand and he put the sketchbook in it.

The sketch was a quick, loose study of me looking off toward the thin horizon. Enough details of the boat were worked in to establish the setting. But the focus was on me. In just a few lines, he'd caught my distraction, my distance.

I handed it back.

"Not bad," I said.

"Okay, this time, look more my way."

I groaned.

* * * *

About midday, we set a course for the Vineyard. "If we power the whole way," Dad said, "which it looks like we might have to, we'll be there around daybreak."

For the first couple of hours, we motored over the lazy swells, the engine humming along. Dad dozed while I steered, then we switched, and I dozed. Then I made some drawings in my sketchbook of the boat and the sail against the sky. I didn't feel like drawing Dad. When I wasn't drawing, I spent most of my time staring out at the water, feeling the immensity of the ocean around us. Here and there I saw fish leap out of the water, even a flock of flying fish skimming and ricocheting off the surface.

A strange feeling came over me as we bumbled through the swirls of the Gulf Stream.

I don't want to leave, I heard my inner voice say. I want to stay. I want to stay out here.

I lay on the cockpit seat and watched the wake churn out behind us, the swells making it rise and tilt as we moved along. I had to admit that I was glad we'd come out here. Who else could say he'd been out to the Gulf Stream? Not even Chet could make that claim. When Beth came back from Italy, I'd have something to tell her I did beside watch Mom drive out of our driveway for good.

When the engine stalled the first time, I thought Dad

was playing a trick on me. In the instant silence that engulfed us I heard the deep gulp of a swell passing beneath our hull.

I looked up at him. I knew by his look that it was no joke.

He hit the starter and it cranked right up. He rolled his eyes and throttled up and we were on our way again.

But not for long. Soon the engine was stalling and coughing more than it ran. Then the breeze died, and the water went glassy.

When the engine quit again, the rigging slatted and slapped as *Piper* wallowed in the slow swell.

Dad checked the fuel level. Then he opened the cockpit hatch and leaned down into the well. He swore, raised himself back up, and wiped at the streak of grease on his cheek. He glanced at me and shook his head. Then he replaced the cover and jumped below. He peered at the manual, licked his finger, flipped pages. He opened the bulkhead hatch and squeezed his way through to the engine for a closer look. He banged on things. He swore. He read the manual again. Sweat dripped off the tip of his nose and darkened his sandy hair. He banged some more.

I heard him throw down his tools with a clang. He peered up from below.

"Try it again," he said.

I turned the key and hit the button and the engine grumbled to life in a cloud of burnt-smelling diesel fumes.

He frowned and looked out to sea as we gained head-way. The helm was easy as we powered over the slick sea.

He wiped his hands on a rag and turned the radio on to listen to the weather. The voice of the weather service forecaster droned out news that got my attention: The low pressure system that only yesterday was supposed to produce rain showers and maybe fifteen knots of wind well to our south was intensifying to a gale and sliding our way.

I glanced at him after I heard the forecast. The only sign that he was concerned was that he lifted his hat and ran his hand through his hair three or four times before he turned to the engine manual again.

Then he came topside and scanned the sky.

"Look at that," he said. Above us, great feathery cirrus clouds had plumed out. He must have been fighting to keep his cool, but all he said was, "Looks like we might be in for a ride. We're going to change our course and head for Nantucket. It's closer."

"Is it going to be a hurricane?" I said.

"No, no. Now don't get yourself worked up. This is just a common everyday low pressure system."

"A gale, they said."

"It might get rough, Luke, I won't kid you about that. But it's no hurricane."

We secured everything as the air grew heavy and the sun faded beneath a canopy of cloud at first gauzy and then dense and dark. In the distance, the water's sheen shifted to a darker color. Nearby the water shivered with cats' paws.

I found myself feeling light-headed, my lungs pumping my head full of oxygen. I stowed lines and shoved gear into lockers. Dad looked in the bilge to find that the water level had risen. He detached the hose from the pump, blew into it and ran a rod through it, reattached it, and started the pump. The level slowly receded.

He finished mopping up the deck and was putting away some tools in the toolbox below. I looked around us as I held onto the tiller. The breeze had begun puffing off and on. We were a tiny boat out in the Gulf Stream, our engine giving us trouble and the seas building. If Dad thought we'd be okay, who was I to say otherwise? But did he really know what to do? If the engine died, if we kept taking on water, then I'd never get ashore. I'd never see Ginnie again. I'd never talk to Mom again. I'd never joke with Beth again. I'd never draw again.

"Dad," I said. "Don't you think that we should call somebody?"

"What's that?" he said as he climbed topside.

"Maybe we should call somebody. For some help."

The engine had been thudding along steadily for a while, but now it began to race. He glanced at me, then reached for the throttle and lowered it. The engine sputtered. He brought the throttle up higher, and the engine smoothed out.

"Why?" he said.

A bigger swell lifted our stern, releasing butterflies inside my stomach.

"The engine," I said. "The storm."

He looked at the sky, at the sea.

"Even if it comes on," he said, "we should be okay. We will be okay."

I wasn't so sure.

"How long would it take the Coast Guard to get out here?"

He laughed.

"They don't come get you unless something's wrong, Luke."

"But there is something wrong. Seriously wrong."

The engine thrummed as if it had always been in tip-top shape, and the wind filled the sail, giving us extra speed.

"Not wrong enough to call the Coast Guard," he said. "You can't call for help every time you hit a few bumps. Calling the Coast Guard is a last resort."

"This seems like more than a few bumps," I said.

He glared at me. "Look, Luke, we don't have to call anybody. We're going to be okay."

Then he smiled and patted my shoulder. "We're almost at the northern wall of the Stream, so we'll be out of the roughest stuff before the storm even gets here. Okay? You with me?"

The waves were looking bigger to me than ever. The wind was coming on.

"I think we should call anyway," I said.

He shook his head. "There's nothing to call about, Luke."

We looked at each other for a moment. Then he smiled again. "Look at it as part of your education as a bluewater sailor. It'll be a notch in your belt."

He looked up at the sail. "Okay. We've got to get a reef in before dark. I'll take the helm now, Luke. You go below and make us something to eat. We might not have a chance for a while. And Luke?"

I stood up, my hands still on the tiller.

"What?"

"We're going to be fine," he said, leveling his gaze at me. "Really."

We switched places at the tiller.

"Okay," I said as I climbed below.

Dad won't call, I thought as I went below. The action of the boat was rougher, and I kept getting bounced against the galley lockers as I scrabbled together a couple of peanut butter sandwiches.

Maybe he was right. We were still under power, and though the wind was building, we'd sailed in higher winds in squalls before. I'd have to trust him, but something didn't feel right. Maybe I was just scared.

Conditions changed fast. The wind came on strong toward dusk. Even after reefing the sail, making it about half its full size, Dad struggled with the tiller.

It was just after dark when the engine stopped cold. Dad hit the starter again. There was nothing but a series of clicks. Without the chugging of the engine, the wind cried and the waves rushed past with the sound of rapids. Dad tried the starter time after time, but the engine was stone dead. *Piper* was heeling over hard in the strengthening wind.

We should have called, I thought, my throat going tight, my mouth dry.

"Time to ride it out," called Dad. "Let's get the sail down. Then I'll see about the engine. Luke, get your life jacket on."

I dug two out of the cockpit locker and tossed him one. I put mine on and pulled the straps snug. Its tight hug didn't comfort me.

Dad brought *Piper* into the wind and we crawled our way forward as the boat bucked over the waves. The sail cracked in the gusts as we fought it down. We lashed it to the boom as best we could.

"I'll get at the engine from below," said Dad. "Can't risk opening the cockpit hatch and taking a sea."

I took the tiller and Dad crawled below. Without the sail, the boat was easier to control even as we bounded over the growing mountains of black water. A strange feeling came over me. We had no power, but my fear vanished. I realized that I was fizzing with excitement. Maybe it was the exertion of striking the sail. The wind moaned in the rigging and I opened my mouth to let it howl through it. Spray splattered me, and I blinked and spat. This was living. This was the thrill. This was the Big Freedom I wanted.

That was when I saw Dad rise up from below. He turned to me, his face appearing in the companionway. He looked at me with an expression that made me catch my breath—a look of blankness, as if he didn't see me.

CHAPTER SEVEN:
THE BROKEN BOAT

A wave crashed over the bow. A ton of Atlantic sea-water charged down the deck, crashing past me to gush through the hatch. I braced my knees against the cockpit as the water rushed around me. I clamped onto the tiller with both hands to keep from getting knocked down. When the water level dropped, I spat out a combination of saltwater and rainwater that poured off the bill of my oilskin hood.

"Dad?" I called. "What is it?"

The water pouring into the cabin brought him around. He wiped water from his face.

"Something's wrong with the main pump," he called. "Got to bail. Try the engine."

I hit the starter button. All that it produced was a watchlike click.

I ducked under the boom, gripped onto the cabin rail as the boat toppled over the crest of a wave, and jumped down into the cabin beside Dad. Cold water pressed up to my knees.

Another wave rolled us over hard. The cabin light

flickered. I bounced off Dad and crashed against the galley stove.

When I stood up, I looked at Dad. He was staring at the water around his knees as if he didn't know what it was.

"Dad!" I said. "What about the other pump? The hand pump?"

He looked at me. Then I noticed what he was holding. It was the handle of the manual bilge pump, snapped off at the fitting.

"Dad!" I said again. "Both pumps shot?"

He looked at me as if I'd said something in Swahili.

I scrambled forward to grab the five-gallon bucket from the forepeak. Already the gear we'd stowed up there had been tossed around.

"For God's sake!" I yelled when I came back. "Will you snap out of it? We've got to bail."

The boat lurched. His eyes focused.

"I'll dump the water," he said, climbing up the companionway steps. "Start bailing and hand me the bucket."

He couldn't blank out any more, not if we were going to make it. He was trying to think of everything that had to be done, I guessed, and he was freezing up.

I plunged the bucket into the water and passed it to Dad as if it were filled with feathers. He emptied it overboard and handed it back.

The boat bashed through the water, the wind and waves battering us. The water rolled and splashed along the cabin floor. Fatigue began to fill my arms like sand. Soon they went heavy and numb and quivery. As much as I bailed, the boat kept on taking on water.

"Dad," I said. "We've got to call. We have to do it."

He looked down at me from the companionway. Spray shot past him as a wave knocked across our hull.

Without saying a word, he inched below and grabbed the handset of the radio.

"Should I get the life raft out?" I said to him. The boat lurched hard over to starboard and he fell against the bulkhead.

. He pushed himself up and lodged himself against the chart table.

"Dad, what about the life raft?"

He looked at me. His eyes widened as if he thought something was going to attack him.

"Dad!" I said. "The life raft! Should I get it ready?"

His eyes focused on me. He nodded.

I climbed topside to pull the life raft out of the locker. I heard Dad talking into the handset of the radio.

"Mayday, mayday," he said. He said the words stiffly, as if his jaw were wired shut. "This is sailing vessel *Piper*. Mayday, mayday." He gave our position and repeated it.

As I opened the locker hatch, another wave broke

over us, filling the cockpit and the locker. I pulled at the handle of the valise containing the life raft. I couldn't get it to budge. Another wave rolled us on our side. Pellets of rain drummed down on me. As much as I tugged, I couldn't free the raft.

Then Dad was beside me. "Hold this," he said over a gust. It was the EPIRB, the emergency radio beacon, a plastic box of electronics about the size of a big flashlight. He hauled out the life raft and unzipped the valise. The raft flapped and fluttered out.

He heaved the life raft over, but part of it snagged on the main sheet and I reached over to free it. When it slid free, a gust lifted the entire raft away from us. Dad was holding onto the painter that you pulled to release the CO_2 canister to inflate the raft. The gust lifted the raft, the painter triggered the canister, and the raft inflated fast. Dad lunged to hold onto it as it went overboard. I reached out for him, but he sailed off with it as if it were a boogie board. I saw him clinging to the raft, his oilskins a yellow glow, his legs in the water, and then he rode up the face of a wave and disappeared.

"DAD!" I screamed as the boat plunged into a trough. I heard him yell, "Over here! Over here!" but when I shielded my eyes against the spray and rain to see in the direction I thought he'd called from, all I saw was black water.

What happened to the EPIRB, I had no idea. I glanced around the cockpit. It had vanished—probably knocked overboard in the scramble to launch the raft. But it was supposed to work anywhere, even in the water.

"Dad!" I screamed. "For Christ's sake, where are you?" The sea returned nothing but the roar of wind and wave. My voice sounded small and tinny.

Dad was gone. I started gasping. I couldn't breathe. Panic rushed up from my stomach to cut off my breath. Dad was gone. I was alone on the boat. I didn't know what to do.

"Dad!" I screamed again. I fell against the rail, my head floating. I kept calling, calling, hearing nothing but the storm. I called and called as the waves crashed against the boat. I couldn't move. My body felt so light I thought I would fly away in the wind.

Then I heard my own voice say out loud, "The boat is sinking. You have to move."

I raised my arms and forced my legs to move me across the cockpit to the companionway and somehow I tumbled back below into knee-deep water.

I had to make myself concentrate, not let myself panic like Dad.

One thing at a time, I told myself. Breathe in. Breathe out. First: Send a mayday. I grabbed the handset and called "mayday, mayday" into it, shouting as loud as I had for Dad. But I blanked on our position. The bearings went right out of my head. All I could do was shout "mayday" over and over. No position, no rescue.

Water surged around my legs. I let the handset drop, the need to find the source of the leak seizing me.

I switched off the main bilge pump. It wasn't doing any good. I was afraid that I might get tangled up with it or get shocked by the electrical system as I was feeling around down there for the problem. I grabbed the bucket and bailed bucketful after bucketful until I was too tired to bail anymore.

"Got to get the water level down," I said. Even when I talked to myself out loud, my voice sounded distant against the sounds of the wind and waves just beyond the cockpit.

Kneeling down on the cabin floor, I pulled up the hatch to the bilge. I plunged my hand down in the water, feeling along the ribs of the boat. The bucking of the boat kept knocking me down and bouncing me off the berths and bulkheads. There was plenty of slime down there. The water sloshed around me as the waves slammed against the boat, low as she was in the water. I edged my way forward, up to my shoulder in the cold water. I kept feeling around for a crack or an open seam, but I could feel nothing other than the slimy wood and the water.

I was wet and cold so I decided to bail some more to warm up. I took the bucket and bailed for all I was worth. Now I could see that bailing had lowered the level. It was only up to my ankles.

"Okay, bilge pump," I said. "Finish it off." I switched it on again, not expecting it to work.

I was looking down into the bilge when I turned the pump back on. At first I couldn't believe what I saw.

"What the hell . . .?" I said.

Instead of sucking water out of the boat, the pump was hosing water into the boat. I plunged my hand down beside the pump itself and felt water pressing and bubbling against my palm.

"Oh, shit," I said. A bilge pump that reversed itself? Was that possible? It was on *Piper*.

I'm dead, I thought as I shut it off and set to bailing again.

Maybe the pump had reversed itself because it had gotten jammed, just like a backed-up toilet sometimes keeps letting the water flow in.

If only I'd thought of this sooner, I told myself as I closed the doors and hatch, I could have figured out how to clear it. I could have stopped Dad from flying overboard with the life raft. But now I didn't have time. The boat lurched and I fell onto the bunk, frozen there for a moment, gasping.

Why hadn't Dad thought of it? Why had he been so quick to abandon the boat? Or had he really meant to?

And then I felt the boat take a heavy roll and lean farther and farther till I tumbled past the porthole.

I grabbed for a handhold and fell into space and things flew around me and I smashed against something hard and the water splashed over me. I landed on all fours on the cabin ceiling. The ceiling was now the floor. Water sloshed around me. Books and pots and pans and canned goods and papers jostled against me. The cabin light flickered and then went off as I got up on one knee and tried to stand up.

"Capsized!" I said. "Knocked down!"

Now the boat might founder and sink in seconds with me caught below in the cabin.

It was dumb luck that I'd closed the doors and hatch seconds before we'd gone over. All of the Atlantic would have poured into the cabin if I hadn't. We would have gone down fast.

The moment I stood up, the boat pitched again, swirling water over me and tossing me and everything else around. The cabin light flickered on again. I came to rest in the bilge, sitting on a book, *The American Practical Navigator*, with the teakettle nudging my knee. Dad's sailing lid was submerged under my foot. I jumped up and splashed my way to the hatch and shoved it open to see what had happened. The cockpit was full of water.

Just astern, another wall of water was rising up. I stared at it as it neared. Our stern rose, rose higher, even higher, but this time the wave didn't break over us. We rode over the top of it.

I grabbed the bucket and went topside to bail out, ducking my head under the boom by force of habit. But I didn't have to. It wasn't there. I looked forward. The mast wasn't there, either. All that was left of the mast was a splintered stump.

"Dismasted," I said. All the rigging, even the forestay and shrouds, had been shorn away. Only the mainsheet block was still attached to the traveler.

"Bail," I said. The boat now took the big swells somewhat more easily. Without the mast and boom, the wind had less of us to knock around. We bobbed like a seagull over the big steep lumps.

As I bailed, it seemed to me that the wind had let up, too. Or maybe it was a lull. Or maybe it was just that it no longer had rigging to shriek through.

I went back below and bailed out the cabin, then closed the doors and hatch and tried to pick up some of the stuff strewn around the cabin. But the boat was still pitching and rolling and swaying and heaving and surging and yawing so much that I couldn't stand up for long, so I crawled onto my sopping berth and gripped onto the frame like a barnacle. I held on while I tried not to think that Dad had panicked and was lost overboard or about my being alone a hundred miles offshore in the Gulf Stream in a broken boat.

The light flickered, went off, flashed on again, then died.

CHAPTER EIGHT:
THE GULF STREAM

Daylight would never come again. How many times I got knocked out of my berth to the deck, I couldn't count. At least we stayed on top of the water, mostly, and we didn't seem to be moving so violently that we'd capsize again.

A million years of blackness passed until one moment when I peered out the starboard porthole to see the three stars of Orion's belt appearing in a break in the clouds on the horizon. They were so vivid and pure and familiar after the density of darkness that I felt thankful to them, as if they could save me.

But the dawn still wouldn't appear. I was shivering and starving but the action of the boat threw me around so much I didn't dare try to dig around in the galley lockers for fear that everything would come flying out. All I could do was hold on in the dark. I lay on my stomach, spread-eagled so I could grip onto the mattress. It was as though the mattress were a raft with me riding it down an endless series of rapids. I shivered in my berth, gripping on as best I could, my mind spinning off in every direction.

I thought of Mom on Little Spruce Island. Probably she was daubing away at a new canvas, humming and mumbling to herself. When she painted, she entered into a kind of trance. Sometimes she kept at it all day and all night. Maybe that was why she took off. Maybe she couldn't stand that Dad and I intruded on her time, even if we didn't think we did. Maybe she wanted to give every second to her painting.

She had no idea what was happening. She probably thought we were tucked safely in Nantucket Harbor. She probably didn't give a hoot about what was happening to us, if she was even thinking about us at all.

Mel would be curled up on Chet's bed, right beside Poppy. He was most likely snoring and farting. Chet always let Mel sleep on his bed. Now I wished I'd let him sleep on mine, too.

Our house would be empty. The smell of oil paint and denatured spirits would still be thick in the air. I pictured the locust trees Mom's studio faced, and the crescent of the cove glinting between them. The house would be silent, waiting for someone to return.

The daylight showing in the porthole was a grayness that gathered while my mind was drifting along with the boat. I sat up. Out the porthole I saw the saving light, the soft gray of a dove's wing, and I could make out the shapes of the big rollers looming past. I caught a glimpse of the dull buff color of the deck. The color seemed so solid and real after the nightmare of darkness.

"We made it through the night," I said out loud, patting the hull of the boat.

But resentment burned up from my guts. I wondered how Dad could have gotten me into this. He didn't know what he was getting us into. He didn't know what he was doing.

The thought of Gus angered me, too. If he hadn't chosen us to tie up to, he wouldn't have planted the seeds of the idea in Dad's mind. Or mine.

Then there was me. I hadn't listened to Gus's warning to ". . . turn around . . . make your way home . . ." whether it was intentional or not. I should've said to Dad, "Let's just poke around Monomoy. We'll head for the Gulf Stream some other time."

And why had I craved the Big Freedom? It was nothing more than another reason I was adrift, alone.

What if the storm had been a hurricane? What if one came up? The only answer was that *Piper* and I would be gone.

Gone the way Dad was gone. Gone because of me. Gone because I had done nothing to save him.

I had to stop thinking and start moving. First, I tried the radio again. The handset dribbled water. It was as dead as the overhead light, as dead as the bilge pump.

All the water sloshing around when we capsized must have cooked the electrical system. At least the pump wouldn't be drawing water into the boat.

I began to quake. I couldn't move. Dad was gone. I looked out a porthole and saw a dark shape pass by. The boat shoved me against the galley locker. Dad was gone and I didn't know what to do. It was my fault that he was gone. My stomach lurched and a clammy sweat broke out on my forehead.

Dead. He was dead. I threw myself onto the berth and drew my knees up and squeezed my eyes shut and gagged with a raging sob. Dead. He was dead. I was dead.

I held my eyes shut and felt the quivering rattle through me and from somewhere outside of myself I heard my voice say, "You cannot panic. You have to move. You have to move. You can't just lie there."

I cracked open an eye to see that the light had grown, and the first thing I saw was Dad's sailing lid in a wet bunch on the cabin floor.

I knew I had to move. Lying in my berth quivering and sobbing about Dad would do no good.

I had to find something to eat. I pushed myself upright, still quivering, and forced myself to the locker and grabbed the first can I touched, a can of beef stew. I hated beef stew but I didn't care. I opened it, found a spoon, and ate it cold.

I searched my seabag for some dry clothes and when I was digging around in the sopping material I felt my cell phone in the baggie. Saved! I thought as I yanked it out, my heart rocketing with excitement. I held it up. The baggie was full of water. The cell phone floated in it like a goldfish. I pulled it out and tipped it. Water poured out. I tried the dripping phone anyway. It wouldn't even turn on. It was fried.

We were far out of range, anyway. I buried it back in my seabag.

The only problem with the daylight was that it showed me where I was. I went topside, bailed out the cockpit, and then grabbed onto the tiller. I took a look around. Huge purply-blue seas with breaking crests appeared as far as I could see in every direction. Winslow Homer's painting *The Gulf Stream* was one I'd grown up with. We had a print of it hanging in the family room, nestled in among my mother's smaller paintings. Homer was one of her idols.

I had become that painting. I'd become the castaway on the broken boat.

I was holding onto the tiller when I heard a different sound, something deep below the sound of the hiss and roar of the breaking waves. It was a low thudding.

The hairs on my neck bristled when I realized what it was: a helicopter approaching.

Maybe the EPIRB had worked after all. Even if it was submerged, it was supposed to send out a signal to commercial and military aircraft showing our position. That's if it worked. I wasn't sure if Dad had ever checked the batteries. If he had, maybe there was a chance that I'd be found.

But what did you do to save him? a voice whispered to me. I pictured him flying off into the darkness as he clung to the raft. If only I had reached out to grab him somehow, grab his arm or leg or a part of the raft, or thrown him a line or raised the sail enough to go after him. If only I had done something beside stand there as if my feet were nailed to the cockpit.

The thudding got closer. When the helicopter approached, the rotors beat the air like a series of monster cannon shots.

"The flares!" I said out loud. If I could find the flares, I could signal the helicopter, even if I couldn't see it.

But the flares were in the ditch kit. The ditch kit was in the life raft.

The helicopter thudded closer. *Piper* swept up the side of a roller and I stood up to see over its foaming crest. In the dim morning light, I saw the ocean spread out before me, an ocean in tumult, all purple-blue mountains with white marbled backs hulking off into the wastes. Far, far off, beyond the wave peaks, I saw the helicopter. It was a Coast Guard helicopter, a Jayhawk, with the orange slash by its nose, its tail tilted into the air as it swooped over the waves with its searchlights on.

Then we dropped down the face of the wave, down, down, and I threw my arms around the tiller and wedged my knees against the cockpit to guide us into the trough without broaching. When we climbed up the face of the next wave, I strained to see what I still heard: the whup-whup-whup of the helicopter, now fading. But I saw only shreds of low purple and gray cloud flying in the sky.

Hold on, I told myself. You've got to hold on. I looked at the waves sweeping past like behemoths that had lost my scent for a moment. They could turn and devour me at any time. The morning light became stronger, but it did nothing to comfort me. I looked up at the flying clouds, and wondered if I could, if I really could hold on.

The sea began to settle as the day wore on. I stripped off my life jacket, glad to be free of its damp weight. I noticed birds were appearing again now that the storm had passed. They were the kind I'd seen when I'd gone fishing offshore with Chet and Bill, birds that only lived on the open ocean. Wilson's petrels, sooty-colored and sparrow-sized with long slender wings, flapped just above the water surface and tiptoed their way toward scraps of food floating by. High-flying gannets with their bandit masks and rocket-shaped bodies dived-bombed into the waves after fish. Shearwaters, looking like compact albatrosses, veered and swooped through the troughs and over the crests. Fulmars, gull-like birds with what looked like an extra half of a beak glued to the top of their regular beak, paddled around the boat and squabbled with each other.

Where they'd gone during the blow, I wasn't sure. I'd heard that flocks of birds sometimes stayed in the eye of a hurricane because it was calmer there. This storm hadn't been a hurricane, but it was rough, and how the birds survived it, I wasn't sure. Still, they'd survived. Now they knew where they were, at home on the water. I didn't know where I was. But I was certain of one thing. I wasn't at home.

I kept the boat pointing north and west as much as I could given the motion of the waves, but there was no telling which way we were drifting. If the Gulf Stream had taken hold of us, and we hadn't been blown out of it, we'd be carried to the east and north, away from land.

I had to figure out a way to turn the boat toward home.

"Make a sail," I said. "What the hell are you waiting for?"

I went below to eat some more stew, drink some water, clean up the cabin, take stock of what supplies I had, and cook up a plan for making a sail. The action of the boat had steadied enough so I could kneel in front of the locker and tally up what supplies I had left:

5 cans of beef stew

2 cans of chicken

3 cans of spaghetti sauce

An almost-empty jar of peanut butter

4 containers of oatmeal

10 gallons of water

4 cans of tuna fish

A box of granola bars

Matches

A box of oyster crackers

Onions

Carrots

Apples

Oranges

Potatoes

It wouldn't last long. Dad wasn't one for laying in too many stores. Even on our other cruises, we never brought a lot of food. He said that "part of the fun is to catch as many meals as we can right out of the sea. We're not out here to get fat, anyway." Beth used to say that we were the only family that was guaranteed to lose weight on vacation. Of course, he hadn't thought that *Piper* and I would be drifting far offshore for who knew how long. We were really intending to hop from harbor to harbor, explore coves and bays, grab meals at restaurants with views of tranquil anchorages and marinas, not to take a detour into the Gulf Stream. For a moment, the crowded bar of The Ropewalk came back to me. How much would I have given to be back there now, jammed among the smokers and laughers and guzzlers, even to have to wait while Dad drank his martinis.

At the chart table, I sorted through the charts and tablets and pencils and found my dad's sketchbook. The table lid had been latched, so water hadn't gotten in. There was a sketch of the boat, of Monomoy as we'd passed it, one of the buoys we'd passed close to, and one of me at the tiller, the bluewater sailor. How ridiculous that sounded now. How pointless getting irritated with him seemed, especially that I'd refused to let him draw me. I'd always liked Dad's drawings but I had to admit that they were nowhere near as accomplished as Mom's or Beth's. It wasn't fair to call him "the Cartoonist," as he said Aunt Lucy had, but his drawings did have the feel of caricatures. No wonder he liked Edward Lear, J. J. Grandville, W. W. Denslow, and N. C. Wyeth. He had a knack for capturing things with the simplest possible line, and he managed to find buyers for them.

I pored over the charts and took a guess where we were: somewhere east of the continental shelf. But since none of our electronics worked and I had no idea how to navigate or fix our bearings, all I could do was keep guessing. Maybe I could figure things out if I saw the stars at night.

The long paddle that had been part of the boat's original equipment was still lashed to the port deck. I tied a pair of Dad's khakis to it to make a signal flag. I found our extra boathook, too, up in the forepeak. The other boathook was in the locker topside. Maybe I could lash them together to make a boom and mast, small though they'd be. I'd read some things about jury-rigging a sailboat, but reading a book and doing it yourself are different things.

And to think that Robin Graham, a guy I'd read about in some of Dad's old *National Geographic*s, had actually sailed around the world by himself when he wasn't much older than me in a little sloop called *Dove*. I was only trying to stay afloat in a soggy catboat called *Piper*.

All day the seas subsided. *Piper* finally stopped lurching so violently and I could move around, keeping only one hand gripped onto the boat (as Dad always said, "One hand for yourself, one hand for the ship"). Down in the cabin, I worked on lashing the boathooks together until afternoon, when the sun broke through and lit the sea so the deep violet-blue, the indigo of the Gulf Stream, glowed around me. I took my flimsy rig into the cockpit. The sun spread its warmth over my back. I hauled some clothes from my seabag, Dad's sailing sweater, and my sleeping bag and mattress into the cockpit to let the sun and air dry them.

Then everything welled up inside me and I cried. Sitting on the cockpit seat, fiddling with my rig, I cried. Hot tears skated down my cheeks. I gasped and snuffled like a kid. I cried because I was scared out of my wits and missed my dad. I cried because I missed Mom, and until now I didn't know how much I missed her. I wished I'd called her when I had the chance. I missed Beth, missed laughing with her like the times we each drew something crazy on different sides of a piece of paper and then unfolded it to reveal some outrageous creation, and we'd almost choke with laughter. I missed Mel and solid ground and trees and dry clothes and a dry bed that didn't try to fling me out of it. I missed hearing someone else's voice.

Crying didn't help, though. It scared me. Was I losing it the way Dad had? Was I going to panic and curl up and sob again, this time without stopping? Would I blubber in the cockpit and wait for *Piper* to sink? Would

I start talking with God and dive overboard? I read a book once about a sailor who did just that, a guy named Donald Crowhurst. On a solo race around the world, he lost it, and drifted around in circles in the middle of the Atlantic, and ended up jumping off his catamaran.

"Get a grip," I said. I looked out at the water and watched the birds flapping or swooping over the swells. I thought of Dad again. I thought of him alone in the raft. He'd be sloshing around, borne along at the whim of the current. If he was in the raft.

Dad was always trying to make me smile, especially when I was feeling blue and just thinking about smiling caused me pain. He had a way of making a lame joke that he thought would force me to crack a smile. But I knew what he was trying to do. I wouldn't fall for it.

Take the day that I told Ginnie about going sailing. Sure, I was feeling freer for the moment, but deep down I knew what I'd done wasn't fair. Later on that evening, after I'd done a lousy job on the sketch of Mel, I decided to go downstairs for a snack. I passed Dad sitting in his chair on my way to the kitchen. Mel was tailing me, hoping for some tidbits.

Dad looked at me as I passed. "Looks like your barometric pressure is about 29 millibars and falling rapidly," he said. "What's got you so low?" I didn't answer him, and what he said didn't amuse me much that night, but

as *Piper* bucked over another wave, I almost smiled—
and I wished I'd smiled when he said it. I wished Dad
were topside at the helm, trying to make me smile. I'd
smile for him. I'd laugh for him, if that's what he wanted.
If we were together, we could laugh together at one
of his bad jokes, and maybe that would fight the fear
spreading from my stomach into my arms and legs.

I shook my head. "Why, goddamnit?" I said under my
breath. "Why did this have to happen?"

The date was August 22, and the days were getting
shorter. The thought of school came to me. It was starting in just over a week. We were supposed to be back
by then. I pictured walking down a hallway and seeing
Ginnie, and the image felt empty, like it belonged to
someone else. I had disappeared. School was so distant,
so alien, as if it would never happen again.

I looked at the water surrounding me.

I had to finish my sail.

The sun was already beginning to lower in the clean
blue sky by the time I'd concocted what looked like a
laughable rig. I lashed the boathooks together with fishing line and stretched a length of line from the end of
the boom to the top of the mast to form a kind of rough
triangle. I wove fishing line through a sheet and secured
it around the line, mast, and boom. I tried to jam the
mast foot into the splintered stump of the old mast, but

I knew it wouldn't stay. I tried wedging it between the cabin hatch and the doors but it toppled over.

I was standing on the cabintop, puzzling about where to set my rig, when a remnant of the storm, a rough lunging comber, swooped under us and heeled us hard over. The rig clattered overboard. I lunged for it and almost went over myself. I jumped below, grabbed the fishing line, and fumbled with a treble hook as I tried to tie the line to it. It was the only thing left that could snag it. I couldn't seem to get my fingers to work. I kept glancing at my rig, which drifted farther and farther away, the buoyant boathooks keeping it afloat. Finally I got the hook tied on and I heaved the line out to try to snag it. I missed three times. The rig and *Piper* moved farther apart, and soon the line wouldn't reach.

I sat down in the cockpit to watch the rig float away. There was nothing I could do about it. I watched it till it disappeared over the long hills of water.

I looked at the sky. "So that's the way it's going to be," I said, realizing that those had been Ginnie's exact words to me.

I held onto the tiller. Night was coming soon, and I was dreading it. I didn't want to be plunged into dark-ness again, to ride the seas blind. The sky was turning lavender and tangerine as the sun sank, and then the sun slipped into the water like a coin into a slot. A few clouds floated off toward the northwest, their bellies lit purple and pink with charcoal gray on top. Soon they went from ice blue to black.

I was scared of the approaching darkness, but it was going to come whether I wanted it or not.

I went below to see if we were taking on any water and to eat some crackers and some stew. I flicked on the overhead light just to see what would happen. Nothing did.

Once the twilight faded, the stars came on as bright as low-hanging chandeliers. Out in the Atlantic, with not even red and green running lights to fill my eyes, the stars and constellations were so bright and clear I almost ducked my head for fear of bumping into them. They were sharp and bright right down to the horizon. Each star showed red and yellow and blue sparkles. The Milky Way meandered overhead like a glowing river.

The thought of another night without the overhead light upset me at first. But the stars were so bright, I could see by them. I didn't even have to force myself to get used to it. And I still had the oil lamp if I really needed it, though the reservoir was almost dry.

Every few minutes I got out of my berth and went topside for a look around. I found Polaris, the North Star, by drawing an imaginary line from the front two stars of the cup of the Big Dipper to it, so I knew where north was, but I still had no idea whether we were heading that way, or any other way. I picked out the Big Dipper and Cassiopeia and Lyra from among the shoals and flocks and schools of other stars. The constellations were familiar, friendly figures that Dad had pointed out to me many times since I was little. They made me think that if I could hold on through the night, I might just live to tell about this.

I scanned the sky and spotted what at first I thought was a shooting star. But it didn't disappear. It was a steady bead of light that crossed the star fields fast and silent as if it were on an invisible rail. I tracked it as it made its transit across the sky. It was a satellite, high and remote, sending its signals to people far away from me.

I went below again, found a flashlight in the chart table, and put on my chamois shirt and Dad's sailing sweater. They felt good after drying out in the sun. Then I got onto my berth. Hundreds of things I needed to do raced through my mind, all of them tumbling over each other to get my attention.

Think up another way to rig a sail.

Read the engine manual to see if there was anything to be done that I knew how to do.

Check the bilge when I got up next time to see if *Piper* was leaking.

Remember to use the fishing gear tomorrow.

I must have plunged into a deep slumber as I ran and reran all the things I needed to do through my mind because when I woke the boat seemed to be almost motionless and a moon like a slice of cantaloupe was rocking in the porthole.

And there was something else.

Out of the silence I heard a sound that made my limbs go weightless. Fear made my guts feel hollow.

Close by, something was taking a bath. Something large. An image jumped to mind of a giant human being lolling in a vast tub, leisurely moving its arms and legs and ladling water over its head. I heard a slow gulp and splash of water and felt *Piper* ride over a small wave.

I forced myself to stand up, grab the flashlight, ease the hatch back, and inch my head out.

Beside the boat rose the silhouette of a great tall fin in the glitter of the moonlight. It glistened as it swung slowly one way, then the other. Its motion pushed out small waves that *Piper* rode easily. No other sound save the splashes came from it. I trained the flashlight beam on it to see a bulbous eye roll toward me and seem to blink. I had been holding my breath, I realized, and now I exhaled when I saw what it was. The owner of the eye was an ocean sunfish, a *mola mola*, a docile creature that looked like a gigantic potato stuck between two

tall fins. It looked as surprised to see me as I was surprised to see it. I knew it was harmless unless we were
underway and struck it. There was no danger of that.
We were both as aimless as the other, flopping around
in the great ocean current.

It finished with whatever it was doing beside *Piper*
and began to descend, slipping away into the dark water.
We were left alone, surrounded by the stars reflecting
themselves on the easy swells, the moon gleaming
on the water. I looked to the other side of the boat to
see the shadow of *Piper* and me stretching across the
water. The sunfish, reappearing on the other side of the
boat, surfaced for a moment through my shadow.

Then it sank into the black water, trailing ribbons of
phosphorescence.

I was alone again. I looked at the immensity of the
sea and sky around me, and I wanted to hide.

CHAPTER NINE:
A DISTANT SPECK

The sunrise was splashing the water with purple and crimson and vermilion flecks when I went topside. The air filled my lungs with its rich fishy saltiness. When I exhaled, my breath puffed out a rag of steam. I wondered how I would go about painting this sunrise, how I could hold onto it, make it mine, and thinking of painting brought me back to the morning before we left when I was looking for my sketchbook. I was always misplacing it. Dad was down packing the jeep, and Mel was following me and whimpering, knowing that packed bags meant he was going somewhere, too. I went upstairs to see if I'd left it in Mom's studio, and when I turned on the lights, I saw it on top of a table full of paint pots. And I saw Mom's painting resting on its big easel in the middle of the room, the one she'd been working on before she'd left.

It was the kind of painting she was known for: an oil of the view out the studio window, about four feet wide and five feet high. It showed the night sky in deep blue gray. Below that was a dark stretch of water, the slice of the cove that she could see from her window. It was charcoal gray. The band of water below that was also charcoal but it had some green worked into it and splashes of white that captured the sense of moonlight glittering on the water. The moon was out of sight, somewhere off the canvas, probably sailing above the top of the frame.

I was always amazed by her paintings. But that morning I couldn't understand why she'd left this one sitting there.

Now that I thought of it, I realized that if she was fed up with us, maybe she was even fed up with the view she had painted so many times. Maybe she no longer felt the need to hold onto that view. Maybe that was why she'd left the nearly finished painting. Would she ever come back for it? Probably not.

I ate a granola bar and an orange while I watched the sun rise. I'd wanted freedom, and I'd gotten it. It wasn't what I expected, but I'd have to live with it—and with the feeling like a hornet stinging the inside of my stomach that I didn't do enough to save Dad.

I tossed the orange peel overboard and wiped my hands on my pants. The sunlight speared peach rays over the ocean. I sat and rocked and stared. Even with no power, *Piper* was seaworthy. I was lucky. But if another storm blew in or I ran low on supplies, we'd be in serious trouble. We might keep drifting on the current and end up off the Grand Banks or Ireland or the Hebrides or beyond. Or maybe we'd get caught in one of the eddies and spin in some endless loop, going around in circles, going nowhere, forever caught in a cycle that would see my bones turn to dust and *Piper* crumble with rot before we would sink to the black deeps.

"Get moving," I said. "Time to go fishing."

I knew I had to stretch my food supplies, so I went below, stowed the sketchbook and took the tackle box topside. We didn't have a pole, but we had two hand-lines.

I decided to fish for a while and hope that a plan for jury-rigging the boat would come to me. I opened the tackle box and picked through it for the right lure. Too bad Chet wasn't aboard. He was as handy as his dad, someone who could fix an engine or bend a plank with ease.

The moment the thought of Dad returned to me, I felt a cold surge of fear. Dad wasn't aboard. The boat felt empty. Picking through the lures, I realized that I didn't know what I was doing, and not just about fishing—about staying alive. If Dad hadn't gone overboard, he'd be here with me now. He'd show me what to do. My hands quivered.

I looked out at the horizon to pull myself together. My hope was that he was alive out there somewhere.

Maybe the helicopter had spotted him. Maybe he was still in the life raft, singing endless rounds of "Dinah won't you blow, Dinah won't you blow, Dinah won't you blow your horn, your horn . . . " to the petrels and kitti-wakes to pass the time.

I managed to tie on a white bucktail with a treble hook and let it plop overboard. The line looped out into the depths. There had been some small fish following the boat and now they finned over to sniff the line, which angled into the water. The bucktail ran deeper and deeper, and soon it was only a white speck. I began giving it a series of sharp tugs, jigging it so it would flash and maybe attract a fish. I felt the fear drain away.

"Here, fishy fishy," I called, mimicking Bill's gruff chant when the fish weren't biting. "Come and take my tasty bait."

The sun climbed higher and the waves glinted as they rolled past without giving us a thought. I was gazing off toward the horizon astern when I heard a slap and splash off to port. I turned to see a dorado jetting out of the water, dancing on its tail, and then plunging into the water again in a great cascade of spray. It was a blunt-headed rocket of a fish that flashed a speckled pattern of aqua and electric yellow and neon green on its sides, and I knew that if I hooked it I'd have a fight to get it aboard. But if I won, I'd be eating one of the tastiest fish in the sea.

Any thought of eating a dorado raw or cooked vanished when the line I was holding jerked taut, almost slicing my palm, and began whipping overboard. I pulled my sleeves over my cupped hands to act as gloves. I gripped back onto the line, and the line yanked me forward. I banged my knees against the cockpit coaming. The line slashed back and forth. Sweat jumped out on my forehead and I pulled back with a grunt. I let the line slither through my hands when whatever it was took off, then hauled back when I could turn it.

Finally it slowed enough to allow me to start heaving it upward. Each pull made me feel as though I'd caught a submarine. I leaned over the rail as far as I dared to see if I could spot it. It felt fierce and strong and fast enough to be a small bluefin tuna. A big one would have towed *Piper* and me off into nowhere. Maybe it was a dorado, though it felt heavier than that and a dorado would have shot to the surface.

Peering into the depths, I followed the rigid line down, down, down to where the lure was. About twenty feet below I spotted what had taken the lure: a blue shark. At this depth it look small, but from the way it felt on the line it must have run close to six feet long.

It gave a great lashing shake that flung my arms back

and forth. It shot off, stripping out line from between my fists. I had a flash of a fantasy of tying the line to the stump of the mast and letting the shark tow us to shore.

"Damn," I said. "Why'd you have to be a shark?" I reached into the tackle box, found a jackknife, and sliced the line.

This was no time to tangle with a shark, all teeth and thrashing and razor-sharp skin.

I folded the knife and put it in my pocket, then wound the remaining line on the handline frame. Fishing would have to wait.

What would Dad do? I asked myself as I looked around the cabin.

On the cabin floor, I found Dad's sailing lid. I picked it up and plopped it on my head. If I was going to be out in the sun, I'd better take precautions, even if it meant wearing the hat that used to make me cringe. In a way, I wanted to wear it now. It was all I had of Dad.

I ate lunch, ladling cold spaghetti sauce out of the can with saltines while I tried to force myself to figure out what to do. I needed a long, strong pole for a mast. I could use the paddle that I'd tied to a pair of Dad's khakis to make a signal flag. I really had no other choice. But what if I needed the paddle and I'd used it as a mast?

I wondered what to use as a boom. I could take apart some of the shelving and lash it together. We had some nails and screws, too, so maybe it was possible.

When I went topside, the handrails on the cabintop caught my eye. If I removed them, I could make them into a mast and use the paddle as a boom. But its area would hold only a tiny sail, one not strong enough to buck the Gulf Stream.

I got the sketchbook and sat down in the cockpit, disgusted with myself at my failure to come up with a solution.

"Draw," I said. "You might as well draw. You're no good at anything else."

What would Dad do? I thought again as I began to sketch the boat, sunlight pouring down out of a sky dotted with puffy clouds. He wouldn't have been drawing, that I knew.

But I did. I made some quick sketches of the boat looking forward from the cockpit. From memory I drew Mel, Gus's boat riding off our stern, our house. I drew Mom walking on the beach on Monomoy and Beth standing in the locust grove the way she did sometimes, leaning against a tree and watching the cove without moving a muscle. Then I drew Dad. I drew him as a shadowy figure at the tiller, the way I remembered him from our trip out, with the starry sky surrounding him and the dark sea stretching beyond. I wished again that I'd drawn Ginnie from life, and why I refused didn't make any sense to me. So I drew her from memory, her face lifted toward mine with that happy expression I'd seen when I was about to bite into the blueberry muffin. But then Cass Garrett took the place of Ginnie, with her ponytail bobbing out the back of her Red Sox cap. I drew her at the helm of the launch, raising her arm and waving at me. I drew as much as I could. I drew as if my life depended on it.

A speck on the horizon appeared and we had been moving toward it for a few minutes before it registered and I stopped in the middle of drawing the curve of *Piper*'s rail. I stared at it, trying to figure out what it was.

It was something orange, something floating, something the same color as our life raft.

I knew that the Gulf Stream ran to the east and north of where we joined it, about a hundred miles off Cape Cod, just beyond the canyons of the continental shelf. All along the main body of the current, parts broke off and formed eddies and curlicues.

Where we were headed when I spotted the orange object I wasn't sure. But the current was taking us toward it.

I grabbed the paddle, my heart pistoning in my chest.

Dad was alive, I thought, alive right there in the life raft. We were drifting toward him. Maybe we'd both been caught in the current's curls and had been spinning around each other just out of view of each other.

I risked standing up on the cabintop to wave my flag. I swept it back and forth as we drifted past windrows of weed, the slow swell now and then rising to hide the raft.

The firecrackers! I thought. If I hadn't thrown them overboard, I could have used them to get someone's attention.

"Get the binoculars," I said. My heart drummed and I realized that I was smiling.

I set the paddle down in the cockpit and jumped below, yanked the binoculars out of their case on the rack above Dad's berth, and ran back topside.

The binoculars were still soaked from falling off the rack when we capsized. I wiped the lenses with my shirttail and nestled them to my eyes.

What came into focus was no life raft. It was a large orange inflated buoy, an orange ball. It wasn't Dad.

I lowered the binoculars, my breathing quieting. Dad had been within reach. For a moment, hope had filled me. I felt my heart slow and my face slacken. My elation leaked away. Now all we were drifting past was a marker buoy.

Then I realized that the buoy was our chance. It was stationary, probably a lobsterman or fisherman's buoy. If I could get *Piper* near it, we could tie up to it. Sooner or later a boat would come to check it. The way we were drifting now, we'd pass close by, but not close enough to grab the buoy.

I tore Dad's pants off the paddle and leaned over the starboard side and paddled, then switched sides, and paddled again till I thought my lungs would rip apart. I was making no headway.

Then I ran below, grabbed the bucket, tied a line to it, and tossed it overboard. A sea anchor might slow us down enough so I could maneuver us to the buoy.

I got the toolkit, nailed the paddle to the stump of the mast, and then started lashing a blanket to it. Maybe I could get *Piper* to react to this rag of a sail.

By the time I got the blanket attached to the paddle, we were so close to the buoy that I could see the water pouring around it as if it were a rock in a river. The buoy vibrated and bobbed in the tide.

I knotted a line to one end of the blanket and pulled.

The breeze made the blanket belly out, and I pushed the tiller so we'd come up into the wind toward the buoy.

But we didn't have enough power. I couldn't get *Piper* to move out of the flow, and the current carried us past the buoy in seconds.

"What the hell is wrong with you?" I yelled at the blanket. I shoved the tiller away from me and ran below again to root around in the forepeak for anything else that might make a bigger sail. All I found was the sail bag.

By the time I got topside again, the buoy had dropped far astern. I hauled the bucket back aboard.

I slumped down in the cockpit and draped my arms over the tiller, exhausted.

If only I'd made some sort of workable sail before, I could have saved us.

It wasn't long before the buoy reached the horizon, rode up one last swell, and disappeared.

As I stared at the empty water, I realized that the buoy meant that we were near fishing grounds. Boats might be nearby. Other buoys might be around. I had no excuse for not jury-rigging a sail. I needed sail power to save myself. No one else was going to help me. If Dad or Gus or Chet or Bill—or Mom, handier in her own way than I'd ever be—had been there, we already would have been sailing. But they weren't with me. I was the only one. I was the only one who could save *Piper* and myself.

I took the blanket off the paddle. With a hammer and chisel, I gouged out a plug from the cabintop so that the paddle would fit into it. I needed to have the mast closer to me in the cockpit.

I tested the engine again, but it didn't even click. The saltwater had drowned it along with the radio and the cell phone and the pump. But an idea came to me, and I stripped off one of its rubber belts.

I went below, found the hammer and a screwdriver, and wrenched out one of the floorboards, a length about six feet long, two feet shorter than the paddle.

I was lucky that the seas were running only about three or four feet, so *Piper* didn't roll too badly.

With the hand drill I cored a hole in both ends of the plank. I fed one end of the belt through one of the holes and then ran the handle end of the paddle through the loops of the belt. The belt, I hoped, would swivel like the jaws on the gaff that was now somewhere hundreds of fathoms below us and miles behind us.

Daylight had almost drained from the sky by the time I'd run a line from the plank end to the paddle top, slit the sail bag to open it up, and lashed it, Dad's khakis, and the blanket with fishing line across the triangular area formed by the line, paddle, and plank.

The stars were already dangling overhead when I made the rig fast to the top of the cabin. I still had work to do on it before I could raise it. I hoped no big wave would wash it overboard during the night. I went below, then poked my head out of the hatch to check on the sail one more time.

Off to port, I saw lights. They were far off, but I knew they were the running lights of a vessel. My heartbeat surged until I remembered I had nothing to use as a signal. But wait: I had the flashlight. I jumped below, snatched it up, ran topside, and began slashing its beam back and forth, back and forth. But it dimmed before long. I kept waving it back and forth and shaking it to coax a yellowish glow out of it. Soon it was dead, and I could only sit in the cockpit and watch.

At first the lights moved fast, and even the distant pulsing throb of an engine reached my ears for a moment. But then the lights slowed, and I saw a brighter white light go on: probably deck lights. The boat stayed in one spot as we drifted away. The moon like an orange fin jutted out of the sea while I watched.

Finally, the deck lights went off, the running lights pivoted, and the boat slipped over the horizon, back toward the world.

I watched the dark line of the horizon for a long time as the moon climbed higher, a white sail now setting a course across the night.

My ragged sail was what would save me, I thought. Tomorrow I would raise it, and then we'd make our own course and if any other boat came near, we'd be seen. If tomorrow wasn't too late.

"Too late," I said out loud, a different feeling building within me. It was a feeling I could not control.

"I have to do everything!" I heard myself shout. Something began boiling over inside me. It shot up like a flame, a blue arc. I felt myself rising up.

"I have to decide everything!" I shouted. "Why? Why do I have to do everything? Why did you take me out here? All of you! You're all goddamn idiots!"

I found myself standing up on the cockpit seat, screaming at the moon. Scorching anger spewed out of me and wrapped itself around me.

"It's all your fault, you bastard!" I shrieked. "Your fault! Yours!" I threw a punch at the moon. "I hate you! Hate you!" I kept shrieking, my voice beginning to crack and rasp. I grabbed the flashlight and heaved it into the darkness. It plunked into the water with a splash of phosphorescence.

I threw punches into the air, screaming, "Damn you! Damn you!" and then I lost my balance, toppling over into the cockpit, banging my ribs against the tiller on the way down.

"You left me," I moaned as I curled up on the cockpit floor.

At last all I could do was whisper.

"Why did you leave me?" I said. "Why did you leave me alone out here?"

For a long time I lay there, the fire finally cooling. My breathing returned to normal. I watched the stars looking down on me, and a calmness spread over me.

I was the same as my dad. We'd both ended up tumbling into the cockpit, making fools of ourselves. Dad had tumbled away from me. So had Mom.

"So this is the way it's going to be," I whispered.

CHAPTER TEN:
SEABORN

I knew I couldn't sleep in the cockpit. I'd get wet, I'd get cold, and I might get tossed into the water. I wanted to burrow away from the openness of the ocean. I wanted to shut out the immensity of the water and the lurching deck and the sight of waves stretching away forever.

So I dragged myself down below. Even though I had no appetite, I knew I had to keep my strength up, so I forced myself to eat another can of stew. Then I climbed into my berth. I kicked myself for not getting the sail up earlier. All I could do now was wait for daylight.

I didn't want to think about the fathoms and fathoms of water pressing against the other side of the hull. We were almost certainly drifting beyond the canyons of the continental shelf, and an image of it formed in my mind. Far below, it looked like one side of a submerged Grand Canyon. Picturing *Piper* bobbing small as a seed above all this immensity filled with darkness and gigantic shadowy beasts made the lining of my stomach go cold and my hands go moist and my breathing go fast and shallow. I had to think about something else.

I couldn't sleep. I felt exposed, as if the world were staring at me. I ached to shut everything out. If I found a good place to hide, maybe I could sleep. There were plenty of cramped nooks and crannies in the boat, but my favorite was the quarterberth. It would be my cave. I could wedge myself in there and blot everything out. I'd be safe.

So I staggered my way past the steps and wormed my way in. I curled up atop a coil of line, some oilskins, a pillow, and other things that had gotten tossed around in the last few days.

Safe at last, I thought. I'm safe in here. *Piper* will keep me safe. I tried to shut out the sounds of the water by singing the words to "Thief" out loud: *I heard you left / Gone to a foreign sea / If love is theft / You stole everything from me.*

When I got tired of my hoarse off-key voice, I rolled over onto my back and stared into the darkness. I knew the ceiling was only inches from my face but I couldn't see it. I squeezed my eyes shut and imagined the time we sailed to Hadley Harbor, and Beth and I were rowing the dinghy to explore the shore, and it was twilight and the water was motionless and we heard ducks quacking and the creak of the oars in the oarlocks and we didn't say a word. I imagined a sunny sky, the kind of sky Dad and I sailed under on our run out to Monomoy, the kind of sky I woke to the morning we left when Dad was furling the awning.

The awning.

I sat up and cracked my head against the ceiling. Stars exploded in my head and I gripped my hand against my forehead.

"The awning," I said out loud. "The awning is in here somewhere. Why didn't you think of it before, you idiot? What the hell is wrong with you?"

Dad must have rolled it up and stowed it in the quarterberth. Then other stuff we tossed in there covered it up. I could criticize Dad for not knowing what to do to save us, and yet I hadn't even remembered the one item that would make the best sail.

By first light, I was topside. I remembered the technique of countersinking from my days working with Chet and Bill. I cored a hole the circumference of the paddle halfway through the cabintop. Then I drove a screw all the way through, took it out, and then fit the handle end of the paddle into the hole. Going below, I drove screws up into the handle through the cabin ceiling.

I pounded several nails through the paddle into the cabintop at an angle and tamped a rag around its base as caulking so water wouldn't leak in. I lashed three lines midway up the paddle and secured one to the foredeck and the other two to the port and starboard rails to act as stays. Then I ran a line through the hole in the end of the plank and through the block on the traveler. That way the plank could act like a boom, and the block would slide along the bronze rod of the traveler when I needed to let the sail out or pull it in.

The wind blew in light puffs from the southeast. I swung the boom out to starboard and pushed the tiller away from me. *Piper* brought her head around through the breeze and pushed over the top of a swell.

I felt the tremble of the tiller and the thrust of the rudder as the wind filled the awning.

"We're sailing!" I shouted. I wanted to laugh and cheer as the line went taut and the sail bellied out and *Piper* eased forward. She was making headway. For the first time in . . . how long? I'd begun losing track of time . . . it was the first time in two days that we'd been under our own power, not the unseen hand of the Gulf Stream.

I could only guess at how far we'd been carried. If the current was running at three knots, and we'd been drifting for around 72 hours, we could have drifted around two hundred miles. But that was assuming we were drifting in a straight line. If we had been caught in one of the Gulf Stream's eddies, we might have been floating back toward land.

Wherever we were, we had to head north-northwest

or west-northwest to hit some sort of land. As far as I knew, we could be closer to Sable Island or Nova Scotia than Nantucket or Cape Cod. Maybe we'd end up on Gus's doorstep.

The breeze remained light and variable all day as we bucked the current. When the sun went down, leaving a turquoise twilight, the moon slid up from behind the earth, and hope rose inside me. We sailed on, making slow progress. I convinced myself that we were on a true course across the Gulf Stream, pointed toward home.

The wind, shifting toward the south, began to build. I put on my oilskins, knowing I was going to get wet. The waves built but *Piper*, even with her awning for a sail, handled them well, climbing and descending their sides. There was a painting Mom had showed me once that came to mind as we pushed over the waves, the moonlight glistening on the skin of the sea, a painting by Albert Pinkham Ryder called *Moonlight* of a small boat with only a rag of a sail bounding through a moon-shot sea.

The farther we sailed the more convinced I became that the helicopter had found my dad, and that when I reached home again, he would be there. I would throw him a line as I eased toward the wharf, and Dad and I would laugh and hug. Flotsam and Jetsam, together again. Lucky Luke and Ahab Andy. And maybe Mel would be there to wag himself into ecstasy and nibble on my ear in joy and relief to find me, hungry and tired and sunburned and salt-stained but happy. And alive.

And somehow Mom would be there, too, hugging me with that fierceness I missed. I could almost smell fresh oil paint.

Piper brought me west-northwest on a course across the Stream. I would make it, I knew. My boat would take me home.

And I knew that something inside me was reborn, born of the sea, seaborn, and like any birth it would leave something of me behind.

As the moon climbed higher, it drew the wind with it. *Piper* yawed over the building waves, the sail slackening in the troughs and cracking full as we clawed up the faces. I gripped the sheet with one hand and steered with the other. My arms shook. When the wind had been light, I had cleated the sheet and looped a line around the tiller so I could rest my arms. But as the wind rose, I had to steer and hold the sheet or *Piper* might broach.

I was in agony. I couldn't feel my fingers. My thighs were sore and numb from sitting on the hard cockpit seat. Clouds raced past the moon, blotting it out and sending the water into shadow. Then the moon pulled free and its light flashed back on, flickering off the hulks of the waves.

I wondered if this was the outer fringes of another storm. I didn't have any idea what the forecast was. Could one have been making its way toward me?

I could not keep this up. The block took some of the pressure off, but hours of holding onto the line had worn me down. I feared that a gust might blow out my flimsy sail. *Piper* unnerved me by fighting to head up into the wind even as we drove up a wave. My only course was to strike the sail and ride out the blow. But I was afraid that I might lose the sail if I took it off the mast. Maybe if I got a few minutes away from steering to relieve my arms and grabbed something to eat for some strength, I could manage to keep going.

Hunger chewed at me. My mouth began to water when I thought of sitting with Mom, gobbling an entire box of warm gooey meltaways. Even Ginnie's muffins sounded good.

I calculated that when we went into the trough of the wave, I had about ten seconds to run below, grab a can of stew or whatever I could lay my hands on, and jump back into the cockpit and gain control of the boat before we topped the wave and the wind caught the sail again.

I looked behind us to gauge the waves. I could see ranks of them marching toward us in the moonlight.

I let the first one rise up behind us and take *Piper* up into the wind. At the crest we heeled over hard and I strained to hold onto the sheet. Then we began to drop. I looked again. The trough seemed to be a long one.

I had to move now. I looped the sheet around the cleat and let the tiller go. I flung myself through the companionway and jumped down into the cabin as the boat slowed in the trough. I banged open the door to the food locker, grabbed a handful of granola bars and an apple, and started back up the companionway steps.

The wave behind us was lunging high in the moonlight, and the sight of it made me freeze. It surged higher, rushing faster toward us. My legs wobbled as I tumbled into the cockpit. *Piper*'s stern swerved away from the wave the moment I reached the tiller and hauled it over to bring us back stern-to the wave. The wave toppled, coursing whitewater down its face with a sizzling roar. Water colder than I expected battered down on me and charged into the cockpit.

Piper wallowed as we reached the crest and the wind hit us, heeling us over hard.

This is it, I thought. I can't keep doing this. The boat can't keep doing this.

We heeled over farther and I let the sheet go. The wind took it with such force that the line whipped across my face, stinging my cheek beside my earlier rope burn.

But I was so absorbed in controlling the tiller to keep us from capsizing that I did not let it faze me. The line cracked and snapped free.

Letting the wind spill from the sail kept us from going over. I snatched at the sheet and got ahold of it to control it. We rushed into the trough and I knew this was the moment. I had to get the sail down and get below and ride out the blow.

We made it through one more wave and I crawled over the cabintop and hauled myself up hand over hand on the mast. I pulled my knife out of my pocket and slashed at the fishing line to cut the awning free. The boat pitched and the awning whipped the air as another wave swept under us. I gripped the awning in my fists and wadded it up as fast as I could so it wouldn't fly off into the ocean. Then I edged my way down the companionway steps, hugging the awning to me. I piled it onto the cabin floor, crawled back topside to lash the tiller, and glanced at the mast against the moonlit sky. I couldn't risk taking it down, not with the boat lurching around so. I was sure it would be swept away in minutes.

I crept below and shut the doors and hatch behind me. I threw myself onto my berth, my body trembling, to hold on as best I could while *Piper* battled the waves.

CHAPTER ELEVEN:
LUCKY STARS

I heard my name as I swam deeper into the blue-green depths, deeper toward a voice calling to me. The deeper I went, the darker the water became. The lens of light at the surface above me began to shrink. In my ears came the distant call, a sound as if a single wave were slowly breaking miles away. In this whisper came the sound of my name. Luke, called the water as I swam through the density of darkness. Luke, said the depths as I saw a single point of light far below. Luke, the voice called again as I swam faster, faster toward the growing pearl of light. And in the light I saw the body of a drowned man, and when I swam closer and the light grew stronger, it sat up and became my father, my father calling my name.

The next moment, it seemed, I was blinking at sunlight pouring in a porthole. Courses of reflected light quivered through the cabin. I was on the cabin floor, still in my oilskins, lying on my back with my hands resting prayerfully on my chest like a corpse in a coffin. The air smelled of cold seaweed.

I staggered to my feet, dizzy from the nightmare,

holding my hands out to balance myself. I was certain that we'd just settled into a trough and that we were about to be launched up on another mountainous wave.

But I didn't need to hold on.

Luck was an ebbing and flowing force that existed as sure as the unseen current of the Gulf Stream itself. It was luck that brought me through the night and the storm. I had been sure I was doomed. I had been gripping onto the sides of my berth, feeling *Piper* lurch and bound and stagger and roll, the sound of the whining wind and the pouring gravel rush of breaking waves in my ears.

Lucky Stars, I thought. It was *Lucky Stars* that brought me to this place, and my dad's string of bad luck.

Sliding back the hatch and opening the doors, I poked my head up to see that the ocean had transformed itself into to a blue-green prairie of long smooth knolls. The air was brisk. The sun shone out of a sky of blue satin.

I turned forward to see that the mast was in its place, slightly cockeyed, but still with me.

I sat down on the top step and put my face in my hands. I was still alive. *Piper* rode the easy swell, the water kissing at her hull. I must have doused the sail at the peak of the storm, and the seas began to subside not long after I'd gone below.

I rubbed my eyes and looked around me. The water had changed color, from indigo to gray-green once again. The air was sharper. Had we passed back into northern waters, out of the Gulf Stream? Or had we been tossed out of a whirl of the Gulf Stream, soon to be scooped up and carried along by it again?

The dream had left me feeling weak and lonely but the sleep had refreshed me, and I felt a new urge to get moving. I was starving, too, and I went below and poured a can of spaghetti sauce over stew, ate it, then gobbled two granola bars, an apple, and an orange. The sea had swallowed the granola bars and apple I'd brought topside before. At last I could eat without banging into things. I knew I shouldn't eat so much since I didn't know how long I'd have to make my supplies last. But the food gave me new energy and hope.

By noontime I'd repaired the mast and rigged the sail again. *Piper* was making headway, pushed by the light northerly breeze. I had to steer more to the west than I wanted, since I couldn't point the boat close to the wind now that it had shifted, but as long as we were moving forward under our own power, I was happy.

But the wind lightened and finally quit by early afternoon. We bobbed on the swell, only a shiver of a breeze riffling the water here and there in the distance. By late afternoon even the shivers of the breeze disappeared.

The water lay window-clear and metal-slick, stretching away to the horizon as taut as cellophane.

I was glad for the calm but no wind meant no movement except for whatever current held us. I watched the water and scanned the horizon as evening came on. Wilson's petrels flapped in the gentle swirls made by the hull as we drifted. Fulmars paddled beside us or flapped off across the water to soar in stiff-winged swoops.

I was watching gannets diving on baitfish in the distance when something flashed into my field of vision and I flinched and ducked my head. I heard a whir of feathers and there before me, on the cockpit floor, was a tiny land bird, a songbird, a tweety bird, way, way off course on his southward migration.

Somehow he'd stumbled on to my tiny island of a boat to rest. He looked confused. He huddled in a corner by a scupper, leaning this way and that with the slow action of the boat, a feathered gyroscope. I picked him up to put him up on the cockpit seat beside me. He was as light as lint.

"Need a place to rest?" I said to him. "How about some water?"

I went below and got a plate out of a locker and poured a puddle of water on it. I carried it topside and set it before the bird.

"You're lost, aren't you?" I said. "Boy, are you lucky you found us."

The bird blinked. I wondered if it was going to keel over from a burst heart after all the exertion of flying over the miles and miles of ocean wastes. It had probably been blown off course by the storm. The bird blinked again, swaying with the rocking of the boat.

"Well, I'm lost, too," I said. "Go ahead. Take a sip of water."

The bird stood on the seat, blinking and ruffling its feathers. I watched it for a long time. I went below and got my sketchbook and drew it. Every now and then, I scanned the water from horizon to horizon. Then I watched the bird, hoping it would survive.

It was while I was watching the bird that I realized I had seen something else on the water in my peripheral vision.

I sat up and stared out at the horizon. An orange speck was out there. It was another marker buoy, I was sure.

But something about it made me think that, if I could, I'd better try to get closer to it. Besides, a solid object out here could mean my salvation. If the current was swirling, maybe it would carry me closer to it.

I played with the line to see if I could shape the sail enough to catch whatever air might be moving. Only a few shivers appeared on the water in the distance, and I felt no air moving on my face.

But the orange object was getting closer. It looked bigger to me than a marker buoy. My heart tripped. I looked harder and held my breath.

Piper drifted, turning slowly with the current. I heard the water licking at the hull. A slight breeze moved over us, enough to sway the sail.

"Come on," I said to the wind. "I need you now."

Piper was making a pirouette on the water, so now I had to switch around to look over the other side to keep the orange object in view.

And then the bird fluttered into the air and whirred away on its bobbing flight. It became a speck that drew my eye along the sky above the water to see that the orange object was what I had been dying to see all these hours, all these days: a life raft, a life raft with a small canopy just like ours.

And in the raft I saw a figure wave his arms, a figure in yellow oilskins and lifejacket, and then raise a paddle and wave it above his head.

The breeze puffed, filling the sail, driving *Piper* forward. The water gurgled around the hull. For a few feet we drove forward, and I brought the bow to point at the raft. But the breeze subsided, leaving the sail limp. We lost all headway and bobbed on the flat water.

I stood up and waved my arms. It must be Dad, I thought. It had to be.

The figure set to paddling again and splashed and flailed for a while before disappearing under the canopy.

Sound travels best over water, and even though we were still far apart, I stood up and shouted, "Dad! Is that you? Dad, it's Luke!"

After a minute I saw the figure rise up again and raise the paddle and slowly hold it up and make a stirring motion in the air.

It was Dad. He was here. He was alive.

CHAPTER TWELVE:
DRIFTING APART, DRIFTING TOGETHER

Just as the sailboats in the Bermuda Race that Gus told us about drifted in different directions, Dad and I must have been spinning around, just out of sight of each other, as the current toyed with us. Maybe my rigging a sail so that I could steer *Piper* on a course broke the spell that would have kept us endlessly twirling around each other without meeting.

The ocean was so glassy and the air so calm I could hear the sound of Dad's paddle splashing in the water. But after another minute or so, he stopped paddling and disappeared beneath the canopy. One minute, two minutes, three minutes, or more elapsed. I watched the drifting raft. It seemed to sit frozen to the surface. Dad did not appear. I kept watching and as I did I could see that we seemed to be drifting apart.

My lungs pumped faster. I looked at the sail hanging slack on the paddle. If I pulled the sail off and took the paddle down, maybe I could paddle the boat to cross the distance between us. But *Piper* was a big boat to paddle, even with such a big paddle. And if a breeze came up, it would be no use. Without a sail, *Piper* would be carried in whatever direction it blew.

I leaped up on the cabintop and shouted, "Dad! Are you okay?"

The raft rested on the water. He didn't appear.

Panic began to rise within me as if I were struggling just below the surface of the water, unable to break into the air. I had to control myself, not get overwhelmed the way I had the night Dad went overboard.

I jumped back into the cockpit and some wild notion made me try the engine again. Nothing. My breathing came hard and fast in my ears, roaring as if I were scuba diving.

"Dad!" I yelled again. "Paddle! Paddle the raft!"

A whisper of air, almost as light as the whirring wings of my bird visitor, brushed my cheek. I turned to see the sail lift, drop, lift again.

"Come on," I said between clenched teeth. "Come on."

On the water surface a riffle swept toward us, and a puff lifted the sail and then filled it. I grabbed the tiller and the line. *Piper* crept ahead, her wake trickling behind her.

I took a deep breath, and in that moment I heard the sound that my rapid breathing was masking.

I searched the horizon one way, then the other, the sound coming to me over what seemed a great distance.

As we inched toward the raft, I looked behind us. I looked in front of us. I looked everywhere for what was making the sound of a distant engine.

At last, directly behind us, I saw the boat, the boat that I had been hearing, the boat with its running lights already on to our north, steaming off at angle away from us.

I couldn't move. Everything was happening too fast for me, just the way it always happened on boats. I was so close to Dad but not close enough. The boat was there but far enough away to miss us. This was the moment and I couldn't move.

But I had to move.

I vaulted onto the cabintop and waved my arms and yelled and jumped and pulled my shirt off and slashed it back and forth. The boat was on a course to the southwest about three miles off. Across the slick water, I heard the hum of its engine. At first I couldn't make out what kind of boat it was, but as it steamed nearer I could see that it was a lobster boat with a few traps stacked on its afterdeck.

I glanced back at the raft. Dad still had not reappeared. Something must have gone wrong.

The breeze puffed again. I jumped to the cockpit to take the tiller and line. We moved ahead toward the raft, and I glanced back at the boat.

It held its course. I saw no one on deck. From my days on *Gloria B.* with Chet and Bill, I knew what fishermen did when they were steaming at sea. The helmsman might check the radar and peer out at the water now and then, but mostly he'd glance at the compass to see that the autopilot was keeping a true course and otherwise stare into space. Anyone else aboard was most likely snoozing. The roar of the diesel would make my screams useless. Only if we were lucky would the helmsman spot us or pick us up on radar. Only then would we stand a chance.

The boat was moving away from us. I felt as though I were losing control. Tears sprang to my eyes, tears of frustration and anger. I screamed so loud my throat went ragged and my eyes hurt.

"Stop, damn it, stop!" I yelled, flinging my shirt back and forth. "Come back! We're here! We're over here! Come back!"

The pilothouse door opened up and someone stepped out on deck. The figure moved to the stack of traps as if to check on something, then moved back toward the pilothouse door, opened it, and paused.

He must have spotted something. Was it us? He stood motionless for a moment, looking across the water. Then he stepped back inside the pilothouse.

I stopped screaming and held my breath. Had he

seen us? Or had he only been looking at something else on the water and missed us?

Black smoke puffed out its stack. Then its bow swung around, and I could see the white curl of its bow wake and its red and green running lights shift position to head toward us.

A laugh burst out of me. It was a laugh that caught me by surprise.

I laughed again, harder this time.

We were saved. He had seen us.

The boat was steaming dead for us.

All I could do was stand, limp now from my frenzy, holding onto the tiller and the line as we closed on the raft. Every now and then I laughed. I was going to make it. We were going to get home.

But what about Dad? *Piper* made straight for the raft, and now I was almost close enough to throw a line to him. I dug a coil of line out of the locker and steered the boat just to the starboard of the raft. We ghosted along, making only a knot or two.

"Dad!" I yelled. "I'm going to throw you a line!"

The raft floated on the rippled water. From the looks of it, it might have been empty. The thought that Dad might have slipped overboard this close to rescue sent a shiver through my blood.

"Dad!" I called again. "Are you okay?"

I turned to check on the progress of the boat. She was coming on fast. Now I could read her name, *Dauntless*, painted under the flared bow.

I brought *Piper* around the raft to see Dad propped up inside, his legs splayed out on the floor. Seawater washed around him. His oilskins were soaked and stained with salt. He was shivering. He turned to me and raised his arm, and his mouth opened but no words came out. His eyes were almost squinted shut and his growth of beard was grizzled with salt and sun. His face was splotched and blistered with sunburn and wind-burn and crusted with salt.

I cleated the line and stood up on the deck. "Here it comes," I called as I tossed the line. It looped through the air and slapped down across his lap.

He groped at it with both hands. He didn't seem to be able to close his fists around it. It began to slip away, slithering back across the raft, as *Piper* kept moving forward. I turned the tiller to try to head into the breeze.

At last Dad managed to grip the line and the raft spun around and skimmed toward *Piper*'s hull. *Piper* slipped past, the raft sliding out behind her stern, until I was able to bring the boat around into the wind. We slowed, and I grabbed the line and hauled the raft up to us.

"Dad!" I said, peering over the rail at him.

He said nothing, but I saw I hint of a smile made by his

blistered and cracked and swollen lips. His eyes were bloodshot and ringed with swollen sunburned skin.

"Just hold on, Dad. There's a boat coming."

Dauntless throttled down as she approached. She was a white-hulled Downeast-type fishing boat about fifty-five or sixty feet long. This close up she looked huge and her diesel roared. She slowed down and came up to idle beside us. The sound of an engine after all the quiet stunned me. *Dauntless* and *Piper* and the raft bobbed on the wake as it slid past. Dad winced with the motion. It must have taken everything he had to paddle when he'd spotted *Piper*.

A man came out on *Dauntless*'s deck, two other men moving up behind him, and looked at me and then down at the raft. Then he pointed to the raft.

"We'll get him first," he called over the mumble of the diesel.

I nodded, gripping the tiller. At first my voice wouldn't work. I opened my mouth, closed it, tried again.

"Okay," I rasped at last, though it sounded as though I were talking to myself.

Now the portside hauling door slid open and the first man worked the boat up to the side of the raft. He tossed a heavy line with a wide loop at its end down to Dad.

"Slip it over your head," he said, "and push your arms through it. We'll haul you up."

Dad let go of the line I had tossed and gripped onto the loop. You could see that he was having a hard time bending enough to get the loop over him, but at last he squeezed through.

The helmsman switched on the pothauler and draped the line on it. The line tautened and eased upward, and gradually Dad was lifted free of the raft floor. Both crewmen moved to the rail and helped guide Dad up the side of the hull. He hung there, limp and dripping, until both men grabbed him and turned him over the rail onto the deck. One of the crewmen ran below, returned with a blanket and draped it over Dad's shoulders. They helped him gain his footing on the deck and guided him below.

The helmsman said, "Catch this," and bent down to pick up the loop. "Ready?" he called.

My throat went tight and I felt my knees weaken. Tears sprang to my eyes. Now I could believe it. Now I could believe that Dad really was still alive.

I waved and he heaved the line. I caught it and made it fast to the forward cleat.

The helmsman brought *Dauntless* closer and the crewmen came back topside. One of them jumped onto *Piper*. He clapped me on the shoulder. "You okay?" he said. "You've been out here a long time."

"Okay," I managed.

I lashed *Piper*'s tiller and climbed below to make sure everything was secure. As I looked around the cabin, weakness floated through me. I wondered if I could hold on. I felt a quaver come into my hands. My legs felt spindly.

I had to get going. I had to see if Dad was okay.

At the last moment, I gathered up our sketchbooks, then half crawled my way back topside. I remembered that I was still wearing Dad's sailing lid. I reached my hand up to it, felt its salt-crusted cloth, and tugged it tighter to be sure it wouldn't fly off.

I stepped to the deck, doubling back when I remembered to close the doors and hatch. The crewman jumped from *Piper* to *Dauntless,* then hauled up the tow line to draw *Piper* alongside. I stepped up, took a deep breath, and jumped across to the rail. The crewman grabbed me and helped me to the deck.

The life raft drifted free, already sailing off on the current to end up wherever the Gulf Stream took it. *Piper* bobbed behind us, riding like a gull on the water.

The helmsman throttled up and swung the bow around to point for home. He was radioing the Coast Guard when I went below to see Dad.

I saw him in the dimness of the cluttered cabin lying on top of a sleeping bag, wrapped up in a coarse blanket, his oilskins, lifejacket, and clothes piled on the deck.

He turned his head to me. He was trembling all over. I kneeled down before him and squeezed his hand. I felt him squeeze back. His hand felt cold and bony.

He whispered something, his mouth making dry smacking sounds. His lips were cracked and swollen.

"What?" I said. He tried again, but I couldn't make it out.

"Could we get some water?" I asked one of the crewmen, and he handed me a bottle.

"Don't give him too much," he said. "Just keep him warm. We scraped up some dry clothes for him."

I set the bottle to Dad's lips. He sipped. Droplets ran down his bearded chin. He gestured for more.

He smacked his lips and wiped his chin with his wrist.

"Lucky stars," he croaked around his thickened tongue, a twinkle sparkling in his eyes. "Thank your lucky stars."

Then he closed his eyes and turned his head away.

"Let's leave him be," said the crewman. "The Coasties will be here soon. He needs to get to a hospital." I glanced at him. The crewman caught my look.

"But don't worry," he said. "He'll be fine."

I looked back at Dad. He'll be fine, I thought. Was that true? At least he was alive. I could see the blanket rising and falling with his breathing. He was right there. But I was afraid. I wanted to be beside him, wanted to hear his voice. I didn't want him to slip away again. My life had come back to me but I knew that at any moment everything could vanish.

"Better let him rest," said the crewman. I nodded, took one last glance at Dad, and climbed the steps to the pilothouse.

"Helicopter's on its way," said the helmsman, reaching up to replace the handset on the radio. "They'll meet us in an hour. You're the two who went missing in that blow at the beginning of the week, right? That your dad?"

"Yes, it is. Thank . . . thank you," I said. "I can't believe . . . I thought I'd never . . ."

"I can bring your boat in for you," he said. "But you'll have to keep her in Nantucket till you get her squared away."

I said that sounded fine. Whatever he wanted sounded fine.

"Name's Sten," he said, extending his hand. "Sten Nelsen." I shook it. It was a huge hand, with a calloused palm as hard as horn. "I'm the skipper of this yacht. Out of Hyannis."

He looked at me for a moment. "Rick will get you some water," he said, "and you should get some rest. Your dad's in rough shape, but I've seen worse. He'll be okay."

He looked through the pilothouse windows, the last glow of the day reflected in his glasses. "Ah, I don't even know if I'll charge you for fuel," he said. "Seems kind of coldhearted, doesn't it?"

"It's only fair," I said. "It's only fair to pay you back."

Rick gave me a blanket to wrap around myself. The other crewman, Pete, who wore an orange watch cap, gave me a sip of water. I began to shiver. I clutched the sketchbooks to my chest.

"Maybe you ought to lie down for a while," said Rick.

I went below to crawl into the berth beside Dad's. His eyes were closed and he was breathing softly. He wasn't shaking.

I was exhausted but I couldn't close my eyes. I lay in the soft berth with the throb of the engine running through me as the boat ran rock solid through the water. But my eyes would not close.

Staring at the cabin ceiling, I saw an image of my mother standing on a boulder, surf foaming white around it, dark spruces behind her, wind waving her black hair. "Why haven't you written to me?" I heard her say. "Why haven't you called? I miss you."

I shrugged off the blanket and went back topside to stand beside Sten. He was a rangy man with long stringy blond hair and a stubble of a beard. He wore glasses with thick salt-speckled lenses. A salt-stained khaki work cap sat at an angle on his head. One of his massive hands surrounded a peg on the wheel.

"Can't sleep?" he said over the engine noise.

"No, not at all."

He looked back out the window.

"We were hunting for some gear in Nygren Canyon," he said. "Lost it in the same storm that caught you. Didn't come up with much of it."

I told him that I guessed we'd been near Oceanographer Canyon when the storm hit us.

"Then you drifted about two hundred miles," he said. "Or maybe more if you've been making your way back to the west under sail. Coasties looked for you. Found nothing, even though they extended their search. Lucky for you Rick went out to check the traps and spotted the raft and your rig. Pure luck."

I sat down on the engine cover, my back to the pilot-house wall. Sten had left the hauling door beside him open so I could see the water sliding past. Cold sea-water flicked onto my face now and then. The light had faded to a faint purple along the horizon, and the first stars gleamed on.

I dozed off. When I woke up, someone had spread a sleeping bag over me. I still clutched the sketchbooks, and I ran my hand over the pebbled cover of mine. A blank page appeared to me, and I watched my hand lay a pencil against its surface to draw out the lines of Ginnie's face. Then the pencil was replaced by a paint-brush, and soon I'd painted her coppery hair and smooth clean features against a sky dotted with pearl-gray clouds. I wet my finger to soften their edges.

I got up and leaned out the pilothouse door. *Piper* followed along in *Dauntless*'s wake. Behind her, I saw the moon coming up from the edge of the ocean.

I felt a rush of sadness that *Piper* and I were no longer alone together. Nothing would ever match our days alone at sea. I had been given the Big Freedom. Luck had brought Dad back to me, and at the same time it had taken a piece of me and left it in the Gulf Stream forever.

But now that I was heading home, I did not want to leave.

On the radio I heard a crackling voice calling *Dauntless*, and Sten replied something that I could not make out.

"They're almost here," he said, turning to me.

I flipped on the cabin light to check on Dad. He turned his head toward me and beckoned me with a flutter of two fingers.

"You okay?" I said, sitting on the edge of his bunk. "You want some more water?"

"No, no," he said. "I want to tell you something."

I looked at him. His beard was rough and gray, his face whipped red and blistered. The skin of his hands was pasty and pickled from the seawater. But his eyes had regained some of their brightness.

"It was me, Luke," he said. "It was my fault."

I had trouble hearing him over the engine noise.

"What?"

"I said it was my fault, Luke."

At first I didn't know what he was talking about. Getting separated at sea was an accident, nobody's fault but fate's, even though I had to grant him that he was the one who'd got us in this mess.

He reached up and gripped my hand. I let him hold it.

He opened his mouth, closed it. He closed his eyes for a moment, then looked at me again.

"I promised myself," he said, "I promised that I'd level with you if I made it."

I didn't know what he meant, but I felt my heart jump.

"There was someone else, Luke," he said, speaking so low I could barely hear him over the diesel. "There was someone else when I went away for that stretch, you remember? When I went to New York last summer?"

I held my eyes on his. I let him hold my hand.

"It was loneliness, Luke. I know that's no excuse. But with your mother, I've felt like I've been alone for a long, long time."

CRAIG MOODIE

He coughed, then wiped his mouth with his other hand.

"There was a woman in New York," he said, talking fast. Maybe he knew that if he didn't get everything out all at once, he never would. "It was brief. It's over. It was over before it began, really. But it happened. I couldn't stand myself afterward. I told your mother what happened when I came home. Confessed to her. Asked her to keep it between us. Begged her. Begged her to forgive me."

All that must have been just before she and I went out to Monomoy.

I wanted to pull my hand away, but I couldn't make it move.

"You can't blame Mom for what happened," he said. "She tried to stay for your sake. Tried to pretend things were normal. But they weren't. They weren't normal even before New York. She didn't understand why I did it. It ate away at her till she couldn't stand it anymore. Couldn't stand keeping it a secret. From Beth. From you. If there's anyone to blame, you're looking at him."

"You idiot," I said before I could stop my tongue. "You mean you almost got me killed, almost got us both killed, because of that?"

He looked away for a moment, then looked back at me. He kept holding onto my hand. I looked out the porthole.

Why hadn't Mom told me? Why had she left without saying anything?

"You can hate me, Luke," he said. "I don't blame you. I'm the one who drove your mother away."

I turned back to him.

"So you're a liar. You cheated on Mom. You lied to me."

I felt cold inside. I wasn't angry. I was numb.

A laugh popped out of my mouth. At last he had succeeded in making me laugh, and it was at something that wasn't even funny.

He was a thief. He stole our lives from us. I had just found him again, and now he was taking everything away.

"Listen to me, Luke," he said, his voice going gravelly. "When I was out there, the water kept filling up the raft. The waves pushed the raft up so high so fast it felt as if I were riding in a runaway elevator, and then we'd slide down the face and it was as though the elevator cable were cut. I don't remember how many times the raft went over and I had to jump out, grab the side, and force it back upright. I knew I was going to die. But I kept thinking of you, how I owed you the truth, and I thought that I had to stay alive, stay alive so I could make things right with you."

He cleared his throat. He still hadn't let go of my hand.

"So I made a promise that I would come clean. Now all I can say is that I'm sorry. It almost killed me to think of you alone on the boat. Or not on the boat, treading water and calling for me till you couldn't tread water anymore. But you did it, didn't you? You made it. You and *Piper* made it. I'll always love *Piper* for keeping you afloat. And you for keeping you alive."

I looked at him. I wanted to tell him that I hated him. But that wouldn't have been the truth.

The truth was that I was glad that he was alive, still glad that we had drifted back together. I had missed him when he was gone. I missed him more than I ever thought I would, missed him so much it almost made me sick, as if I had nothing but blackness inside. How could I hate someone I had missed so much? I couldn't. I couldn't because he wasn't the only one. There was Mom, too. Their lives had drifted together, once, and then they drifted apart. I couldn't hate him for that.

"And then when I saw the boat," he said, now in such a low tone that I had to lean close to hear him, "I thought I was hallucinating. It couldn't be true, I thought. And then I saw you. My boy. My boy, alive."

He gripped my hand harder. I looked at him. I wasn't sure if I was smiling or grimacing.

Through the portholes I saw a flash of white light.

"Must be the Coast Guard," I said.

"Luke," said Dad. "You don't have to forgive me. I just wanted you to know the truth."

I nodded.

"Better go on deck," I said.

I helped him up. He draped an arm around my shoulders. He felt flimsy, almost birdlike. We hobbled up the steps into the pilothouse to see the helicopter's searchlight probing around to locate us. It was a Jayhawk helicopter, maybe the same one I'd seen before, and its thundering beats grew louder than the sound of the boat's diesel.

Sten throttled down and told Pete and Rick to go out on deck. As the helicopter maneuvered to hover overhead, beaming its light on us, the rotor wash flattened the water out in planes of spume and spray. The helicopter rode above *Dauntless*'s afterdeck and lowered a basket in the cone of light. We bundled Dad into it.

His eyes held mine in the flashing light as Rick and Pete strapped him in. I knew what I was going to do. I reached my hand out and squeezed his and pointed with my other hand toward *Piper*. He moved his eyes to where I was pointing, then looked back at me and nodded. The basket teetered, and then it rose into the light.

I looked from *Piper* to the belly of the helicopter hovering above us. The basket twirled upward.

A crewman gathered Dad into the helicopter, then leaned out and gave us the thumbs-up.

"All set!" yelled Rick over the roar. "You're up next."

I glanced at *Piper* riding off the stern. Even with the roar and whine of the helicopter, the world seemed quiet to me. I knew I had to stay with *Piper*, the boat that had saved me, to shepherd her to shore. I owed her that much.

I shook my head. "Staying aboard," I yelled, pointing at the boat.

He nodded and gave the crewman another thumbs-up. The crewman waved, ducked inside, and shut the door. The helicopter banked, swooped low over the water, then climbed for home, making a thudding whup-whup-whup as it headed away.

After the roar of the helicopter, the diesel seemed hushed.

I went back into the pilothouse and stood beside Sten. I could see the lights of the helicopter diminish over the water.

"There he goes," he said. "He'll be in clean sheets in Falmouth Hospital before we see the lights of Nantucket. They'll take good care of him."

"Once I get *Piper* squared away," I said, "I'm going to be with him."

Sten nodded. "We've got a few more hours of steaming

ahead. You should try to get some rest. Rick'll fix you something to eat."

"Thanks," I said. "I'm just going to check on the boat first."

I stepped past the stack of traps and made my way to the stern. *Piper* was cleated fine. I leaned my thighs against the rail. The prop wash surged out and the wake sizzled out behind us. *Piper* cut back and forth on her line, a silhouette in the glittering path of the moon.

Beyond her, beyond the thin horizon, was where we'd been, where we'd almost been lost.

Lost. Was Dad lost? Lost in his own confusion? I wondered if I could ever really forgive him. Or if Mom could. There would always be this between us.

I thought back to the time Cass had invited me for ice cream. If I'd gone to see her that day the weather was foul instead of loafing around the boat, I could have changed what happened. Maybe. But not what Dad had done.

And if I'd called Mom that night, would she have told me why she left? Would that have changed what happened?

Would luck bring Mom and me back together, the way it had with Dad?

All I knew was that now we were heading home.

I felt the slight rise and fall of the boat on the smooth swells. Dad would be all right, and I felt a pang that I was not with him. I felt a pang, too, looking back at my boat as she cut back and forth behind us on her tow line.

But she was not lost. She had made it. She was the reason I had made it—the reason both of us had made it.

I pictured landing in Nantucket. I'd tie up *Piper* and make sure she was snug. I'd set foot on the wharf, and it would feel to my sea legs as if it were swaying under me. I would smell sand, flowers, cooking. I'd hear crickets, cars, music, laughter. I'd see lights and faces and trees and fireflies.

Maybe I'd make my way over to the launch dock, if I wanted. Maybe Cass was there. We could have that ice cream.

When I got home, I'd hug Mel and let him sleep on my bed. I'd listen to that CD of Beth's, over and over. And I'd make that drawing of Ginnie.

I looked out at the water. Again I saw myself on Nantucket, walking over the cobblestone streets to the phone booths I'd passed before, the ones on Union Street, the ones I could have used to call Mom.

The image was a signal. I turned around and made my way forward to the pilothouse.

Mom would have known. She had been waiting. She would be waiting now.

Sten nodded when I stepped inside. I went to the radio.

"Okay if I use this?" I said to him. "I have someone I need to reach."